YOURS ALWAYS, MASON

Yours Always: book 1

RYENNE RENNER

Yours Always, Mason

Ryenne Renner

Editing: C Hinkle

Cover Design: Smokey Boy Designs

CHAPTER ONE
Ronnie

Ten years ago...

"Ronnie! Are you ready?" My mom's voice echoed up the stairs.

"Not yet! Just ten more minutes!"

I glanced in the mirror for the millionth time. The pale blue dress was floor length, the sandals were strappy and black... I'd gotten my hair curled into perfect dark brown ringlets that reached the middle of my back. Simple was best. I applied some dark brown waterproof mascara around my light hazel eyes and an extra coat of clear lip-gloss. Perfect.

"Ronnie! Mason is here!"

Perfect. I wanted to see his face when I came down the stairs. It didn't matter that we'd been dating since the seventh grade. Mason's smile when I came into view was a constant in my life. It never failed.

So many people had told us it wouldn't last. I was captain of the volleyball team; he was captain of the chess team. Why didn't I date a jock? Why didn't he go out with one of the other nerds? One of my friends had compared us to Jughead and Veronica. But it didn't matter because we were best friends; had been since we were four and my family had moved next to his. And besides, this was real life. This wasn't a movie where the jock chick was drop dead gorgeous and the nerd boy was all awkward with bucked teeth and glasses. I was actually the one who wore glasses. Thick ones too. Contacts were the best invention ever. And Mason? Mason could have modeled underwear and made a killing. Those natural dark brown curls, those light green eyes... and that ass.

I grinned. That ass belonged to me and I couldn't wait to see it in a tux.

"I'm coming!" I called out.

Tonight would be a night to party it up with our friends and say goodbye to grade twelve. Summer was going to be the usual with summer jobs and campfires. In the fall, we were heading to university. I was going to be a teacher and he was going to be a computer analyst.

I admit, I did the whole cliché walk down the stairs for a big reveal. But it wasn't Mason who was shocked. It was me when my eyes found him at the bottom of the stairs, his eyes glued to the ground.

I stopped midway down the stairway and frowned.

"Mason? Why aren't you dressed?" I wasn't mad. I was worried. Changing plans without letting me know was not something Mason Trenton did. Ever.

He looked up at me, his eyes red, and my heart dropped.

"What's wrong? What happened?" I looked from him to my mom who shrugged and shook her head, her eyes showing she was just as confused and worried as me.

"Can I..." He ran his hands through those amazing curls and cleared his throat. "Can I talk to you?"

The excited butterflies in my stomach turned to nervous ones.

I nodded.

He held his hand out to me and I took it, letting him lead me across the street to the park.

Sitting on the play structure, he kept his eyes on his knees. Teardrops fell on his jeans leaving dark blue spots in their wake. I put my hand on his knee, scared.

His hand covered mine, his other arm brushing across his face. "I have to go," he whispered.

"I don't understand." I swallowed hard.

"My family. We're moving."

My chest started to hurt. "What? Why?"

He shook his head. "They weren't going to let me say goodbye." He glanced back at our houses. "But I couldn't just leave and not tell you."

"Mason. What's going on?" My tears were flowing just as freely as his and he reached up to wipe them away.

"I'm not allowed to say."

"When will you be back?"

He shook his head.

"Never?"

His silence was answer enough.

"Well, where are you going? You need to phone me when you get there!" Sobs shook my whole frame.

"I can't." His arms wrapped around me held me close. I returned the embrace, needing to feel him while I tried to process what was happening.

"I don't understand," I whispered.

"Mason!" We both looked back at the sound of his dad's voice.

"I have to go." He dug into his pocket. "I... I was going to give you this tonight. You know. Just a promise that I'll always love you."

He pressed something into my hand and closed my fist around it. His lips found mine. The kiss was urgent, rough, desperate.

He pulled away, leaving me breathless and reeling.

"I'll always love you." His voice broke. "I'm so sorry, Ronnie."

And with that, he jumped off the play set and sprinted to his family's SUV which was waiting on the street. I watched him punch the door before opening it, his fist leaving a dent.

I didn't notice the rain start to fall as the vehicle swallowed him whole. I didn't notice my mom running toward me as the SUV drove away.

I watched as the taillights disappeared around the corner before looking down at the perfect silver band with the green gemstone in my hand. *Yours Always, Mason;* he'd gotten it engraved. My stomach heaved and I doubled over, my stomach emptying in the sand.

CHAPTER TWO
Mason

Two years ago...

I watched as Bear adjusted something on Pointer's vest then gave his twin a pat on the arm. Pointer nodded and they turned to me.

Pen and Pup came to stand beside them.

I made sure the knife on my leg was strapped in. "Alright guys. This one should be basic, but let's not get too comfortable. We all know things can go to shit in a matter of seconds. The area has been cleared. So, in and out. Simple. Fast. Pointer and Pen, you'll cover the entrances. Bear, you'll cover our backs. Pup, you're with me on explosives."

Everyone nodded and we jumped into our vehicle.

I liked these assignments. Just a quick demolition of ex bases or hideouts so they wouldn't be used again. No killing. No being shot at.

It didn't matter how safe the op was, though; I always sent up a wish into the universe that everything would go well and that it would bring me one day closer to being with Ronnie again.

I let myself think about her as we bounced down the trail to our objective. I knew she'd become a teacher. Of course she had. She'd always been amazing with kids. By the looks of things on her social media the last time I'd risked going online, she'd just left that useless dick, Carl. He was the third boyfriend in the eight years since I'd left. It killed me every time it happened. It made me want to start a profile and say, hey! But, I couldn't. Not yet.

So I secretly watched her and yes, I knew how creepy it was, but I needed to make sure she was safe. It was why I stayed away. It was why I kept an eye on her from afar. She needed to be safe.

Pen pulled to a stop not too far from the building and we all piled out.

Everyone strapped their helmets on.

"Alright. In and out," I repeated. "Two, two, five."

Two minutes to get in, two minutes to set the charges, five minutes until detonation.

Pen nodded, her green eyes bright. She loved this shit. She broke left and Pointer went right.

Bear, Pup, and I moved past him into the building.

Two minutes started now.

I pulled my pack off my back, pulling out everything needed. Pup went left. I went right.

Two minutes...

Meeting back in the middle, Pup gave me the thumbs up and I nodded.

Five minutes...

The numbers ticked off in my head. It was automatic. I didn't even think about it anymore. I had a silent stopwatch in my brain.

"Sneak..."

I frowned and looked back. "What are you doing? Let's go!"

He shook his head and disappeared into a hallway to the right.

Three minutes...

I heard a sob and saw Pup carrying a kid. There was no way that kid was more than eight years old. What was a kid...

Pup grunted and the kid screamed as he fell to the ground.

"Contact!" I barely managed to get the warning out before I felt the bullet go through me. "Everyone out!"

Another shot rang out, this time one of ours. My shirt and pants were warm with my blood and I pulled myself up.

"Pup!"

I saw him push himself up, grabbing the kid, motioning for me to go. I turned, getting almost out before realizing something was wrong.

He wasn't behind me. Where the fuck was he?

Bear's eyes met mine before I raced back in.

Pup was down. He wasn't moving. The kid wasn't moving. We had to go!

I stepped towards them and I hit the ground again, my legs giving out.

"We gotta go, Sneak!" Bear's voice barely registered.

What were we at? Two minutes? No. One minute? A minute was plenty of time. We could do a lot in a minute... but we didn't have a minute.

I didn't hear a noise. All I felt was the pain.

The last thing I remembered was Ronnie's face and the soul crushing feeling that I wasn't going to get to explain to her why I'd left.

And everything went dark.

CHAPTER THREE
Ronnie

Present...

"Now, class! Who can tell me what six plus two equals?" I grinned as eager hands shot into the air. "Jacob!"

"Is it eight, Miss Regnier?"

"It IS eight, Jacob! Good job!" I clapped and the rest of the class followed suit.

The bell rang and all the kids put their books away before getting ready to head home. I stood at the door and waved goodbye as everyone left.

With a sigh, I went back to my desk and got my things ready for Monday.

My phone vibrated one quick vibration and I dug it out of my purse.

Nel: **Are you out of there, yet?**

I laughed at my phone. **No. Jesus, the bell just rang. School still lets out at 3:20 just like it did ten years ago.**

Nel: **Well, hurry your ass up and get to my place. I already opened a bottle of wine!**

I grinned. **Okay. I'm running home to change then I'll be right there.**

A knock on my door had me looking up into Tim Aston's dark brown eyes. I managed to hold in my groan. Now, don't get me wrong, the sixth-grade teacher was hot. He'd also slept with most of the other female staff, even some of the married ones. I was pretty sure I was the last one to hold out since he'd been getting persistent about going on a date the past few weeks.

"Hey, Tim."

He gave me a half smile which had been kind of sexy at first. Now it was just getting to be creepy. "So, any big plans tonight?"

"Actually, yeah. Girl's night."

"Feel like some company?"

I raised an eyebrow. "Not unless you magically turned into a woman."

The muscles in his jaw ticked.

"I have to go. See you on Monday." I slung my purse over my shoulder and closed the door as I walked past him.

"Well, if you change your mind…"

"I won't!" I called back over my shoulder. "Ever," I grumbled under my breath.

My thumb automatically found the ring on my right ring finger like it did every other time I got stressed. Considering that ring was a representation of the most devastating day of my life it was sort of strange how the movement calmed me.

Getting in my jeep, I tossed my purse on the passenger side before starting it up and heading home. Once there, I put on a red flowing top with spaghetti straps and a pair of dark blue jeans. Looking through my shoes, I settled on some dark grey wedge sandals.

Flipping my head upside down, I added a bit of hairspray to keep the bounce and finished off the look with a second coat of mascara and sheer lip-gloss.

I picked up my phone. **Almost ready.**

Picking up the mail I'd brought in, I leafed through it while I waited for her answer. Bill, bill, junk... an envelope with my address handwritten on it caught my attention. Taking a deep breath, I opened it. My heart dropped and yet I sighed in relief as a thank you note fell out for a donation I'd given to a local charity.

Not a letter from a ghost.

Nel: **I'm at the bar. Britt text to say she was already here.**

Ok. I'm leaving the house. I'll be there in five.

Grabbing my ID and bank card, I put them in my pocket then left my apartment, walking toward the bar.

"RONNIE!"

I glanced around, trying to pinpoint where Nel and Britt were screaming my name from.

"Hey!" I sat down, glad the girls had already ordered me a drink. I took a sip of my beer and sighed. "How was your day?" I asked over the music. I loved this bar. There was no DJ, no band, just a jukebox. The best thing about this jukebox was the music selection. There was everything on there. It made for fun and varied nights.

Britt rolled her eyes. "I swear, if I have to listen to one more asshole tell me how to change the oil on their car, I might just kill someone." She shook her head wildly, her tight black curls bouncing around her. Her dark skin was flushed, either from the alcohol or anger. I was going to go with both. "Like seriously. You bring your car to a mechanic to get the oil changed and when you see it's a woman going under the hood, you decide you know how to do my fucking job? I can't wait until Roger's is rebuilt from the fire so I can leave this drive through oil place. Then I can go back to working away from idiot eyes."

She scoffed and took a long pull from the straw in her rum and seven. "Assholes."

Nel and I repeated the word, agreeing.

"My day was fine," started Nel. Her blond hair was short and spiked, her light blue eyes rimmed by layers of black eyeliner. "Work was good. We shut down early because it was slow. Then I got home and remembered my wife fucking cheated on me, so it was a little downhill from there."

She smiled as we each put a hand on her arms. "Thanks. But now? Now, I am fucking fantastic! Because I am here with my girls, and we are going to dance the night away!"

"Woooooooo!"

We all lifted our drinks and gulped them down as the next round showed up.

Nel cocked her head at me. "And you?"

I smiled. "Good. The kids were all angels today." My mind flashed to the mail.

Britt's brow creased. "What?"

I shook my head. "It's nothing. I just had a moment."

Nel put a hand on mine, not needing an explanation.

"I was opening the mail. There was a handwritten letter. I thought... How is it that ten years later I'm still so fucked up about it. Like, I wanted it to be from him saying, 'hey! I'm back!'. And then, on the other hand, I'm still so pissed I'm pretty sure I'd hit him if I ever did see him again."

Britt took my other hand. "He was a part of you for fourteen years, Hun. He was your best friend. The love of your life. Of course, you still miss him."

Nel nodded. "That doc you were seeing said it would take time."

I sighed. "I know. And I try not to think about it, but very once in a while, I can just see him, living his best life, everything perfect... and I'm not a part of that."

Nel grunted. "Repeat to me what else the doc said."

"Not to try and visualize what his life is like because I have no idea." My heart dropped. "For all I know, he's not even alive anymore." The thought nearly brought tears to my eyes. God, I was a mess, flying from one end of the emotional spectrum to the next when it came to Mason. Stupid thank you note. I'd barely thought about him for over a month and here I was again. The worst part was the not knowing.

Taking a deep breath, I took a drink and smiled. "Tonight, we're going to bitch out misogynist men, get over cheating wives, and forget about long lost boyfriends."

My friends grinned and agreed.

Britt frowned. "Ronnie, did you invite that gorgeous teacher friend of yours?"

"I... what? No!" I looked back at the entrance and groaned. "What the hell! He tried to invite himself along and I said no. I didn't even tell him where we were going."

The chair beside me scraped back and that creepy half grin was in my face.

"Ronnie! Fancy meeting you here!"

I raised an eyebrow, not bothering to hide any of my annoyance at his presence. "How did you find us?"

"What? No! I just happen to like this bar." His good humor started to falter as my frown turned to a glare. "Fine. I asked Teri where you like to hang out. In my defense, I asked her two weeks ago."

"I told you it was a girl's night. I told you you weren't invited."

"Right. But now I'm here, so.... why don't we have a drink? I'm sure your friends would love me!"

Nel scoffed. "I'm a lesbian."

He turned his attention to Britt.

"I'm straight, but right now, I really fucking hate men. So, no."

I shrugged. "Sorry. This is a no men's allowed table."

I almost felt bad for him as he stood, clearly displeased, and headed to sit at the bar.

Britt leaned forward. "Okay. I know you said he was getting pushy and creepy, but what the hell!"

Nel nodded. "That's starting to hover near the stalker line." She looked towards the bar and gave a slight shake of her head. "Did you guys notice there's a couple of guys with earpieces in? Do you see anyone important?"

I glanced around. "What? Where? They're probably just on Bluetooth or something. No one important comes here."

"Yeah. You're probably right. One more thing... your stalker is pounding drinks like they're saving his life, so you're coming to my house tonight. I don't need him following you home."

"Awww, I love you too," I answered, grateful for the two women in front of me.

Some older song with a good beat came on and we got onto the dance floor. I was having a blast, the stress of the work week washing away in sweat and booze.

Until I felt a pair of arms wrap around my waist and pull me to the chest attached to them. I pushed away and turned.

"Tim! What the hell! I said I'm not interested!"

"Oh, come on. I've seen how you look at me!" He was starting to slur. He tugged me to him again and tried to kiss me.

I pushed off of him again. "I look at you like you're my coworker. I do not want to date you!"

People on the dance floor had stopped dancing, watching. My girls stood at my back, ready to give whatever kind of support I needed.

"Who says I want to date you. I just figured you'd be a good lay," he mumbled as he reached for my arm again.

Before I could react, he was screaming in pain, his arm twisted at an uncomfortable angle behind his back. I watched, stunned, as a pair of cuffs snapped around his wrists.

"The lady said no."

The voice slapped into me, and I forgot to breathe. I knew that voice. It was deeper and a little gruffer, but I knew that voice. My eyes snapped to the man who had come to my rescue. Those light green eyes met mine and I swallowed hard.

"Mason?"

He licked his lips in the exact same way he used to do when he was nervous all those years ago.

All those years ago…

Anger flared. Where had he been all this time? What the hell was he doing here now? Why was he wearing an earpiece? And, oh my god! Did he know what he'd done to me when he'd left?

Ten years of pain, heartache, fear and worry came to a head in that instant.

"Ronnie, I..."

Whatever he'd been about to say stuck in his throat. I pushed him back with all my strength. Jesus, he'd gotten taller. And thicker. And...

"Ronnie, stop." He tried to grab my wrists, but even I could tell he wasn't trying very hard. He just let me hit him, over and over.

The body wrenching sobs were back. The ones that had kept me in bed for months after he'd disappeared.

"Sneak? You good?"

I barely registered the other man now standing beside Mason.

Mason nodded, his eyes never leaving me. "Ronnie, you can keep beating on me all you want, but let's do this outside before someone here decides you need a night in the drunk tank."

I was so focused on hitting him, I didn't notice we were making our way out of the bar until we were standing in the night air.

My hands hurt. My arms hurt. My heart hurt.

All my emotions collided with the adrenaline. My stomach heaved and I puked.

All over Mason.

CHAPTER FOUR
Mason

I sat on Ronnie's couch in my boxers and t-shirt, waiting for my pants to dry in her dryer. Her two friends sat across from me, glaring daggers. Bear and Pointer stood off to the side, clearly enjoying my misery. So much for brothers sticking together. Traitors.

"She's been in there an hour," whispered the blonde to the other girl.

There hadn't been any introductions and any time I opened my mouth to try and make conversation, one of them cut me off and told me to zip it.

There was a knock on the door and Bear let in our fourth. Pen walked into the room and took in the scene. She grinned.

"Cute outfit," she teased. She shook her head and rolled her eyes. "Pervert is at the police station. There were enough witnesses that it was a non-issue. I didn't even have to bat my eyelashes at the cop."

Bear grunted.

"What? I could bat my eyelashes if I felt like it!" Pen grinned and brushed the long dyed red hair out of her face, her green eyes sparkling.

She went to stand by Bear and Pointer. As always, she looked tiny beside them. Most things did. Topping out at 6 foot 6 inches, the identical twins were a wall of muscle with short dark hair and dark brown eyes.

Much to the dismay of Ronnie's friends, Pen helped herself to the fridge and pulled out enough beers for everyone.

"Since tonight was a bust, we might as well take a break," she announced.

I shook my head as she offered me one. I needed to talk to Ronnie. Standing, I was quickly flanked by her friends.

"I need to talk to her."

The blond grunted. "You had ten years to talk to her, Mason."

My name rolled over her tongue and I realized I knew her. In high school she'd been the funny girl everyone got along with. She'd moved to town in grade five. Ronnie had immediately dubbed her her best friend. She'd lost a lot of weight, the hair was different, the makeup…

"Nel."

"Oh. You do remember me."

"Of course, I remember you."

She raised an eyebrow at me.

"Fine. It took me a minute but come on. You look nothing like you did ten years ago."

"Yeah, well, it's amazing how accepting yourself can improve your mental and physical health."

I waited to see if she was going to elaborate. Instead, she glanced at the bedroom door.

"You fucking destroyed her when you left."

I swallowed hard. "I know." I cleared my throat. "I need to tell her what happened."

"Why now? What's it going to change?"

"She'll know I didn't want to leave her. She'll know it had nothing to do with her. I was a kid, Nel. I didn't have choice."

"You could have told her why."

"No. I couldn't. But I can now." I closed my eyes and blew an exasperated breath out of my nose. "Nel, please."

I glanced at the other woman in front of me. This one I was positive I didn't know. "I'll go in. If she kicks me out, I'm out."

"Nel..."

"Britt! What the hell? United front, man!"

Britt glanced from me to Nel. "Look, I wasn't there for the immediate carnage, but I still helped pick up the pieces when we all met a year later."

Her statement nearly killed me. A year later? She'd still been a mess after all that time?

"I say let him go," Pen piped up. "She's not the only one who's a mess over what happened. You might be friends with her, but we're friends with him. And what happened fucked him up pretty good."

Nel's hesitancy slipped a notch.

"Please." My chest tightened and I took a few deep breaths to keep a mess of emotions from bubbling up. Losing my shit right now was not going to help my case.

"Nel."

Everyone looked at Ronnie who was standing in the doorway. If I'd had trouble breathing before, the ability to suck in a breath completely disappeared that instant. She'd changed into a plain black t-shirt and red checkered pajama pants. Her hair was still down, the long dark waves falling around her shoulders. She'd taken out her contacts and was wearing her glasses. Those amazing hazel eyes met mine and it took everything in me not to rush over to her and crush her to me.

"It's okay, Nel. He can come in." The statement was so quiet, I wasn't sure I'd heard it before she turned and disappeared back into the bedroom.

I froze. I'd thought about this moment almost every waking moment in the past ten years. Hell, I even dreamed about it. But now, the moment was here. There were no more hypotheticals, no more being able to reword things if they came out wrong...

"It's now or never, Sneak." Pen was watching me, all joking aside. "You've survived being shot and blown up. What's the worst that could happen?"

Ronnie's friends gawked at me.

The worst that could happen... that would be Ronnie not understanding. It would be her pushing me away... It would be her doing to me what I'd done to her all those years ago and disappearing. Because one look at her in that bar had been enough to destroy me all over again. Her telling me she couldn't forgive me? I didn't think I'd survive that.

CHAPTER FIVE
Mason

I was kind of glad when Ronnie didn't look up as I walked into the room. I paused and took her in, sitting on the edge of the bed, her hands in her lap.

I made my way over to her and sat beside her. My mind flashed back to the night I had said goodbye.

"What happened?" she whispered.

I watched one tear freefall onto her leg, then another.

Taking a deep breath, I went straight to that day. There was no beating around the bush. Might as well just rip off the Band-Aid. "My dad turned evidence over on one of his clients. It turns out he was bad. Really bad. That day, around lunchtime, I found Roxie in the kitchen. Her head..." My stomach rolled as I remembered finding my dog. "She didn't have a head."

I swallowed hard and closed my eyes, trying to find another image to focus on.

"We went into witness protection. We weren't allowed to tell anyone. I..." I cleared my throat. "I wasn't allowed to tell you. It wasn't safe to tell you."

I glanced at her and found her looking at me.

"After we left, my dad didn't want me to stay around in case they found us. I enlisted. I got trained as an analyst, but it turns out I'm really good in the field, too. I deployed and then I deployed again. And again."

I inhaled deeply. "They found my mom and dad."

"Mason..."

"Please." I shook my head. "Just... just let me get it out."

Her hand settled on my leg and my heart kicked.

"I was on an op when it happened. That was five years ago." I kept concentrating on her hand on my leg. "I was told the man responsible was shot by police."

I held my hand over hers, scared she'd pull away if I tried to take it. She turned her palm up in invitation. My heart kicked as I laced my fingers with hers.

"I came back two years ago. That's when I learned the man who killed my parents was still alive. I'd thought of finding you, but with him still out there... I couldn't chance you'd be a target, too." I ran my thumb over her hand, willing her to believe me.

"And now?"

"I've been tracking him and I got a lead. He's here, Ronnie. He was supposed to be at the bar tonight, but he never showed."

"So, you're not here for me, then." Her voice was so quiet just like it always was when she was hurt.

Once again, I was the reason she was hurting.

"I knew you lived here. I knew I might run into you." I shook my head. "I wanted to run up to you in the bar. Christ, it took everything in me not to. I was scared."

"Of what?"

"Of putting you in danger. Of being the reason something bad happened to you. Of how you felt. I was scared you hated me for leaving. I couldn't handle it if you hated me, Ronnie."

CHAPTER SIX
Ronnie

"I couldn't handle it if you hated me, Ronnie."

His voice cracked with the admission and my heart broke along with it. Whatever it was I'd thought he'd been doing the past ten years, none of it had come close to what he'd just told me. Well, maybe the whole witness protection thing had popped into my head a couple of times, but I'd quickly brushed it away. There was zero reason whatsoever they'd be in a position like that. His dad was an accountant. His mom was his dad's secretary. It was a small family business...

But I'd been wrong.

"I could never hate you, Mason." I looked at my hand in his. His hands were rougher, more calloused. There was a scar on the top of the one I was holding. I looked up his arm and saw a couple more. A tattoo peeked from under the sleeve of his t-shirt. I wondered what else his shirt was hiding.

"Are you okay?" he whispered.

My chest clenched at the worry in his voice. My heart pounded. I had so many questions. There were so many emotions.

I leaned into him and he wrapped his arm around me.

My initial angry phase was over and relief was starting to win out. He was alive. By the sounds of it, he'd been through hell, but he was here. My heart skipped.

"I can't believe you're here."

"I'm here, Ronnie. I'm so sorry."

The tears were still flowing, but now, they were mostly happy ones. His cheek rested on the top of my head. He smelled the same. He still held me the same way. He felt different, but so familiar. He was taller, thicker... solid. He still felt perfect.

It had been ten years, but even after all these years, he was my home.

The adrenaline started to wear off and I yawned. My yawn set off his.

Without a word, he lay down, pulling me to his chest. I wrapped my arm around his waist and his lips found my forehead.

In this moment, no more words were needed. Obviously, we had much to talk about, but for tonight, it could wait.

CHAPTER SEVEN
Ronnie

I slowly came to and glanced toward the window. The sun was shining through the crack in the curtains.

I stretched and Mason groaned as the motion moved me away from him. His arm reached for me and pulled me back to him. It was the ultimate flashback to when we'd fall asleep together, only this time, one of us didn't have to sneak away to stay off the parents' radars. Thinking back on it now, I was pretty sure our parents weren't as clueless as they'd pretended to be.

It should have felt strange, lying next to him, yet it was anything but.

"Mason."

He grunted.

"Mason, I have to pee."

I felt him smile against my shoulder.

"Fine," he whispered.

I got up, opened the bedroom door, and stopped short.

"What's wrong?"

I shook my head and grinned. "They're so cute," I said softly.

My open concept apartment was littered with sleeping bodies. One of the twins, I wasn't sure which one, was sprawled on the couch. His brother was on the floor. Britt was curled up in a ball on the easy chair while Nel and the woman with the bright red hair lay snuggled on the loveseat.

My back warmed as Mason came to stand behind me. He chuckled.

"By the looks of the beer bottles, we missed quite the party."

I glanced back at him, noticing the scar on his left cheek and another over his left eye. I reached up and traced them.

He closed his eyes briefly then gave me a small smile.

"I'll make coffee," he offered.

"Okay."

His fingers traced along my jaw and I couldn't hide the shiver that ran through me. Blushing, I went to the washroom while he headed to the kitchen.

Good lord, I felt like I was in middle school again and Mason had just kissed me on the cheek behind the slide on the playground. I tried to remind myself I was being an idiot. I hadn't seen the man in ten years. There was ten years of history I had no clue about. Last night, he'd been sweet and apologetic. He'd run into me and had taken the opportunity to explain himself. This was him being considerate...

My heart dropped and I swallowed hard.

A soft knock on the door pulled me out of my thoughts.

"You okay?" The worry in Mason's voice made my anguish worse.

"I..." I cleared my throat, hating myself for my loss of control. Ten years later, I was standing in the bathroom just as devastated as I had been all those years ago.

"Open up."

"I'm good. I just need a minute."

"Ronnie. Talk to me."

I opened my mouth only to be betrayed by a sob. A few seconds later, I heard him pick the lock on the doorknob.

I turned away quickly, trying to wipe the tears from my face.

He closed the door and locked it again. His hands touched my shoulders and slowly turned me to face him.

When I didn't say anything, he picked me up by the waist and set me down on the counter. And just like he'd done many times before so long ago, he wrapped his arms around me and let me cry.

He smoothed my hair, rubbing my back, his chin on my head.

I wasn't sure how long we stayed that way, but eventually, I ran out of tears.

Staying between my legs, he reached for some tissue and gave it to me.

"You're going to finish whatever it is you're here to do and then you're going to leave again," I whispered, keeping my eyes on his chest.

He stiffened. "If that's what you want."

I frowned. "You said..."

"I said I had to catch him and I was scared to come back into your life until that was done. He knows I'm after him. He doesn't have the protection he had when he killed my parents. He'll use whatever means necessary to get me to back off. That includes hurting those I love."

My heart kicked. Those he loved.

"There are four people I give a shit about left alive, Ronnie. Three of them are sleeping out in your living room." His hands cupped my face, his thumbs running lightly across my cheeks. "The other one is you."

"It's been ten years..."

"Ten years that I've been trying to find a way to be with you again." He pressed his forehead to mine. "I have loved you since I was four. My parents taking me away... that didn't put a stop to how I felt." He took my hand, his fingers playing with the ring he'd given me.

His words sank in, and I tried to process it all. All this time I had given up on him, he'd been trying to keep me safe until he could come back to me.

"It took me years to find a semblance of control again, Mace. That night... it almost killed me." Did I still love the man? Absolutely. But my past ten years had been spent much more differently than his. While he'd been finding his way back to me, I'd been concentrating on moving as far away from his memory as possible. "I can't just…"

"I know." His fingers ran through the hair just behind my ear and I shivered.

How did he remember exactly where to touch me after all this time? Because he was Mason. Because this was the kid who had done research on how to make a woman come before our first time because he hadn't wanted me to be disappointed.

"I'm not asking you for more than you're ready for. I'm back, okay? I'm here. Whatever you want, however you want…"

My brain was telling me I was being an idiot for believing he wouldn't break my heart again. My heart was trying to remind me it hadn't been his fault he'd left. And my body? My body was starting to melt into his touch, wondering if after all this time he'd still do that thing with his tongue…

A knock on the door made me jump.

"We gotta go, Sneak!" Pen's voice came through the door. "Rat has some info."

"Shit." Mason hung his head back. "Okay. I'll be right there." He looked back down at me, his light green eyes searching mine. "Will you have supper with me?"

"Tonight?"

He nodded. "Here? I'll cook."

I stared speechless.

His face fell. "It's too soon. I get it."

"No! I just... you cook?" I laughed, remembering how he used to burn spaghetti.

He smiled and my heart melted.

"What time?" I asked.

"I'll come at five."

"Okay."

His grin widened. "Yeah?"

"Yeah." My heart was pounding and the butterflies were crashing around in my stomach.

He pressed his lips to my forehead before opening the door. Pen tossed him his pants.

"Let's go, lover boy. You know Rat doesn't stick around if we're late."

"Bastard better have a good explanation why we came up empty handed yesterday," grumbled Pointer. "This should have been fucking over."

Bear grunted.

Mason stopped short as they reached the door. He turned back. "Do you have a pen and paper?"

I found the notebook and pencil I kept on the coffee table.

He scribbled something down and handed it back. "That's my cell."

I nodded.

"I'm leaving, but I'm coming back."

I blushed. Again. Good lord, I hadn't blushed this much since high school.

"Jesus Christ, man. Just kiss her and let's go!" Pen checked her watch. "We've got twenty minutes to get across town."

The blood rose up his neck. I kissed my fingers and pressed them to his cheek.

"Go. I'll see you tonight. Be careful."

He nodded and I watched him walk out the door.

CHAPTER EIGHT
Ronnie

I turned and found Britt and Nel staring at me. "What?"

Nel's eyes widened. "What do you mean, what? What the hell happened last night?"

"I..." I ran my hands over my face. "I don't even know how much I'm allowed to tell you guys."

Britt scoffed. "All of it. You think it's going to go any farther than this living room?"

I took a moment to think about it. These girls had been the reason I was still here and a functioning adult.

"I'll give you the short notes."

They nodded.

"Witness protection, military, his parents were killed, and now he's trying to find their killer."

"What the fuck..." Nel shook her head in disbelief. "Are you for real?"

"Yeah. Jesus, it sounds crazy when I say it out loud."

"So, that's why he left and why you couldn't find him." Britt grunted. "That's some crazy movie shit."

"Are you okay?" Nel put a hand on my arm. "That's a lot to take in."

"I... yeah. It's nuts. But I'm alright. He... Nel, I don't even know how to explain it. We just sat there and talked, and it was like he'd never left." I blew a breath out of my nose. "I mean, there's marked differences. His voice is deeper, and he's got scars and at least one tattoo and, oh my god, did you see the size of his arms?" I laughed.

"Shit. Never mind his arms. Did you see the size of those twins?" Britt was grinning.

We both turned to Nel.

I smiled. "So... the redhead..."

"Pen. Her name is Pen." Nel's blush flooded her face. "Don't judge me. I was a few beers in, and she was hot."

We all laughed.

"No judging." I gave her a hug. "You deserve some fun." My stomach growled.

"Oooh! We should go for breakfast." Britt was already pulling her hair up into a clip before heading into my room where each of them kept a couple of night after outfits for when girls' night got a bit too much fun.

"Yes. Let's." I made my way to the bathroom to put my contacts in. I remembered how Mason had held me just moments earlier and I smiled. Was it ridiculous to be so happy when I still had no idea what was going to happen? Probably. But in this moment, I didn't care.

CHAPTER NINE
Mason

"You guys are assholes," I grumbled as we traveled in the black SUV with tinted windows.

Bear grunted and I rolled my eyes at him.

Pointer didn't bother arguing my point. "We might be assholes, but you'd better get your fucking head in the game if you're going to stay alive long enough to enjoy having her back in your life."

I clenched my jaw. "You think I'm not fully aware of what could happen here? I stayed away from her for ten years to keep her safe. And all of a sudden, the bastard ends up in the same town as her? Trust me, I'm not an idiot. That's not a coincidence."

Pen glanced at me from the driver's seat before concentrating on the road again.

"I don't know how the hell he found out about her, but if he even comes close to touching a hair on her head, he's not going to see a pair of cuffs. I will rot in jail before she gets hurt because of me and none of you will try to stop me." I met three pairs of eyes. "Are we clear?"

"Yes, Sir." Pointer nodded and the other two followed suit.

Pen pulled into an empty parking lot and a nervous man wearing a baseball hat low over his face jumped up from where he was sitting on the hood of his car.

"Before you get pissed, I have no idea what happened. He was supposed to be there. The girl said that's where she was meeting them." Rat's bloodshot light blue eyes flicked nervously over all of us. He looked exhausted and I didn't care.

I ground my teeth together, trying to get my anger in check. I had to remind myself over and over… I wasn't mad at Rat. I wasn't mad at my team. I was pissed the bastard somehow knew about Ronnie.

"Why that bar?" I inquired. "Why did he pick that one?"

Rat shook his head. "No idea. She said they started hanging around there about a month ago."

"You told us you found him a week ago," growled Pointer.

"I did! They did!"

"Which is it, Rat? A week or a month?" Pen took a step towards him and he flinched despite the fact she was almost a foot shorter than him.

"A week!" Rat squeaked. "A week! She told me her boyfriend had been taking her there for a month. I didn't know that was relevant! A week ago, your man showed up."

I pulled five hundred dollars in twenties and fifties out of my pocket and waved it in front of him. "Find out what else she knows, Rat."

He nodded quickly. "I will. I will. Promise, boss. Promise."

Jumping into his car, he squealed away from us.

"This is bad, Sneak." Pointer's comment was echoed by Bear's grunt.

I ran my hands over my face, trying to put pieces of the puzzle together. We'd brought down six dangerous criminals since we'd gotten back home. It was all about puzzles. It was all about putting pieces together until you caught the bastards... but this one, the most important one... none of the pieces fucking fit.

Bear's hand touched my shoulder and broke my train of thought. I looked up and watched his hands.

"You're right. Someone needs to sit outside her place. I'll talk to her tonight about setting up cameras and an alarm system."

He nodded.

We might have had a lot of puzzle pieces that weren't lining up, but one thing was obvious. There was one important piece, and that piece was Ronnie.

CHAPTER TEN
Ronnie

I grabbed a beer out of the fridge and looked over at the mountain of a man sitting on my couch. I smiled, remembering the surprise on Bear's face when I'd tapped on the passenger side window of his SUV. He'd looked up at my Jeep still parked in its spot and raised an eyebrow in question. I'd explained I'd walked to the store to grab a few things then invited him to come up.

I handed him the water he'd asked for and sat on the loveseat before taking a drink of my beer.

"Is it because of the man you're trying to catch? The one that killed Mason's family?"

His dark brown eyes met mine and he nodded.

"Should I be worried?"

He started to shake his head reassuringly then stopped. His head nodded.

My stomach dropped. "Will Mason explain it to me tonight?"

Bear nodded.

"Ok." I tried to think of something else. "How did you meet Mason?"

He took a small pad out of his pocket. **We got put on the same team overseas.**

"You guys weren't just regular military, though, were you."

He shook his head.

"Are you sure you don't want a beer?"

He shook his head. **Can't drink on duty. Sarge will have my head.**

"Who's Sarge?"

Sneak.

"Mason is your sergeant?"

He nodded.

I just stared at him, letting the information sink in. My eyes moved to his throat and the scaring there. My hand moved to my neck unconsciously.

"I... I'm sorry. I didn't mean to stare."

He gave a small nod, encouraging my question.

"Is that how you lost your voice?"

He nodded.

Sneak can tell you about it.

"Why do you guys call him Sneak?"

He grinned.

He's a sneaky bastard. Can get into any building without anyone seeing him. Can also hack into any computer system out there without being detected.

He underlined 'sneaky bastard' a few times to emphasize his point and I laughed.

"What about the rest of you?"

Pen: mightier than the sword. Our first op, a crazy guy with a sword came at her. She took him out with one well-placed punch.

Pointer: like a laser pointer. Sniper.
Bear:

He shrugged.

I'm good at ripping things apart. Things = very bad people.

He watched me as I read the note and I realized he was waiting for my reaction.

In the little amount of time I'd spent around the twins, I'd noticed two differences. One, was the scar on Bear's throat. The other was their energy. Where Pointer was light, Bear was dark. I had no doubts the man intimidated, even maybe scared some of the people he came across, yet I somehow knew I had nothing to fear.

I nodded to show I understood and he relaxed, a small smile on his lips.

He always talked about you. Actually, meeting you is kind of weird. We all thought maybe he'd made you up. You know… Just picked some random chick on social media to be his fake girlfriend.

He grinned and shook his head in disbelief.

"So, he…"

"Ronnie!"

I jumped as Mason hollered my name and pounded on the door.

Bear was up so quickly I almost wondered if he'd been sitting. He put a hand up to get me to stay put and strode to the door.

It wasn't until he reached it that I noticed he'd pulled a handgun out of somewhere. He peered in the peep hole and opened the door, his one arm blocking the entrance.

Mason stopped short as his chest hit the massive arm in his way. His eyes met mine, the fear in them obvious. He also had a gun, his pointed at the ground.

He turned to Bear who'd grunted.

Bear nodded at Mason's gun and put his own away in the holster his button up shirt had been hiding.

Mason took a few deep breaths before doing the same.

Bear let his arm fall away and Mason's long stride ate the distance between us, his arms crushing me to his chest.

"You're okay," he mumbled into my hair. "I thought you weren't okay…"

"Mason. We're fine. What's wrong?"

His head snapped up and his gaze homed in on his friend. "Where the fuck is your phone?"

I watched, awed, as Bear signed what he needed to say.

"Who the hell forgets their charger? And you just forgot to text me from her phone…"

Bear's hands danced some more.

Mason gawked. "You forgot because you still can't believe she's actually real?" A few choice words filled the air before he turned to me. "And you?"

"Me, what?"

"Where's your phone?"

"Charging in my room. I must have left it on silent mode."

He ran his hands over his face, clearly frazzled.

"Mason." I put a hand on his arm and he relaxed slightly.

"I just..." He turned to Bear. "I'm sorry." His next apology was to me. "I couldn't reach either of you and Lukas wasn't in his truck..."

I glanced at Bear and mouthed Lukas as a question.

He shrugged.

I turned back to Mason and took his hand. "We're okay."

The tension fully left him.

"Is it five already?"

He nodded.

"Do you need help bringing anything in?"

"Um, no. I'm good."

Bear nodded his farewell as he followed Mason down the stairs. I looked out the window and watched as they talked about something, Bear signing his side of the conversation. Mason gave Bear's arm a pat, and the big man got in his vehicle, driving away with a wave. Mason went to a second black SUV and pulled out a few bags of groceries.

I let him in and watched as he pulled things out to put on the counter.

"So, are you allowed to have a beer, or are you on duty, too?"

He smiled. "I can have one. Bear could have had one, too."

I popped the top off and handed it to him. "What are you making?"

"Fettuccini alfredo with shrimp skewers and bacon Caesar salad. Oh, and parmesan garlic bread."

"I'm... wow. I'm impressed."

He grinned and my heart stuttered.

CHAPTER ELEVEN
Ronnie

Supper had blown my taste buds away. Mason had turned into one hell of a cook sometime in the past ten years.

"That was amazing."

We'd spent the majority of our time eating and blurting out some of our favorite memories from our childhoods.

Mason laughed. "Do you remember that time when we were ten and we got stuck in Mister Hall's apple tree?"

"It's a little hard to forget. The man threatened to shoot us out of the tree with his shotgun!"

"I'm pretty sure the only reason he didn't was because I fell out and broke my arm."

I scoffed. "Every year, those apples went to waste just because he was a cranky old ass who hated kids."

He grinned and my heart kicked.

"I still think I might be dreaming," I admitted.

He gave a small chuckle. "Honestly, me too."

His look softened. "So, do you like being a teacher?"

I nodded. "It's amazing. I've been teaching third grade for four years now and I love it. It's definitely my favorite age group."

"How are your parents?"

I smiled. "Good. Still living at home. Dad took early retirement. They spend the winters traveling and the summers at home."

"Have you told them?"

I shook my head. "I... I wasn't sure if I was allowed to. I thought maybe you'd want me to wait until you caught that guy."

His relief was obvious. He nodded. "Yeah. I didn't really have time to ask you not to, this morning. As soon as this is done, we can tell them. Or you can tell them."

He frowned.

I put my hand on his. "We'll tell them."

His smile was everything and there was a flutter in my chest.

"Why did you pick Granger Springs to teach?"

I took a second to think about it. "Well, I guess because it's still close to home so I could still go visit mom and dad on a weekend if I wanted. And, I don't know. I liked how small it was. Britt is from here and let me know about the opening at the school. Nel didn't have much of a plan other than she wanted to open a flower shop so she followed me here."

He nodded.

"So, uh, Bear says you showed them my social media..."

He grumbled something about Bear dying the next time he saw him. "It's creepy. I know. I just... it was the only way to check on you to make sure you were alright."

"I wish I'd found a way to see yours," I admitted.

He shook his head. "I don't have any. Not under any of my names. I couldn't take that chance."

I frowned. "How many names do you have?"

"I was Shane Malcolm after that first night. When I enlisted, they changed it to Wayne Ouellette." He took a deep breath. "When mom and dad were murdered, I changed it back to Mason Trenton. I guess by then I didn't care if he found me. Or maybe I wanted him to..."

He looked up when I took his hand.

"I'm so sorry, Mason." I had to clear my throat. His poor parents.

He offered me a sad smile.

"So, if you're you again, how come I was never able to find anything about you anywhere?"

His smile turned cocky. "I have decent knowledge of how the internet works and how to make it work for me."

"I believe the term Bear alluded to was something along the lines of master hacker."

He laughed. "Is there anything Bear didn't tell you?"

"He told me to ask you about how he lost his voice..."

His good humor vanished and he sat back, his hand pulling out of mine.

Shocked by the anguish I saw on his face, I made my way to his side and hugged his head to my chest, my lips on his hair. Whatever had happened had caused fear and absolute devastation to pool in those perfect green eyes.

"It's okay. Not today. Not ever if you don't want to," I whispered. What in the world had he been through?

"Come on." I took a step back and offered him my hand.

"Where are we going?" He frowned.

"Nowhere. You're going to lay on the floor and I'm going to rub your back like you used to love."

His lips twitched. "Yeah?"

"Yeah. Come on." I pulled him up and led him to the living room.

He kneeled, hands taking a hold of the hem of his t-shirt. He hesitated before pulling it over his head.

My chest squeezed and my hands flew to my mouth to keep myself from making any audible sound.

I saw him tense before he dropped to the floor, his head face down in his arms. The scars I'd noticed on his arms and face were nothing compared to the ones on his back. I didn't know how I knew, but those scars had something to do with Bear's voice and the terror in Mason's eyes.

I straddled his hips taking the lotion from the coffee table. I squirted a few pumps on him.

He jumped under me. "Still haven't learned to warm it up first?"

"I haven't given many back rubs in the past ten years. And besides, I told you. I like to watch your muscles flex when I do that." And holy shit, did those muscles do amazing things now that he'd filled out.

I used my thumbs to work the lotion into his skin, loosening the knots as I found them.

He started to relax under me. I took my time, taking in all the ways he was different with the scars and tattoos. The one I'd seen peeking from under his shirt sleeve was a gorgeous dragon, its tail wrapped around his arm, its body taking up most of his side and back, flames shooting across to cover the right shoulder.

Different, but also the same with how his head rolled to the side the more he relaxed, and his mouth opened as he got lost in my touch.

I traced my finger along one of the longer scars and he tensed. "Do they hurt?" I whispered, fighting the urge to cry.

"No. Not anymore."

I softly kissed one scar then moved on to the others, letting my fingers trail along his skin. Once I started touching him, I couldn't stop. The ten years we'd spent apart vanished.

"Roll over," I said softly, needing to look into those eyes I'd missed so much.

I took in the sight as he did like I'd instructed. More scars. A tattoo of two butterflies with dates under them for his parents. One of Veronica and Jughead kissing along his ribs. I smiled. That one was us.

"You have chest hair."

He burst out laughing. "Jesus, Ronnie. Out of everything, that's what you notice?"

I grinned. "Well, you didn't have any last time I saw you like this."

"I'd barely hit puberty the last time you saw me."

I let my eyes trail over him. "Puberty is a good look on you."

I touched the tattoo that represented us. "I can't believe you're here," I whispered.

"Every day since that night, I've been trying to find a way... but you had to be safe." His hand pressed against mine over the tattoo.

"But you don't think it's safe yet."

He shook his head.

I swallowed hard. "I don't care."

"Ronnie..."

"No. I don't care. You can't leave me again."

His hand caressed my cheek.

"Promise."

He nodded. "I promise."

I closed my eyes as that part of me who knew him better than anyone else heard his words, heard the emotions behind them, and the really crappy walls I'd put up around my heart when I'd seen him in the bar crumbled.

Leaning down, I brushed my lips against his and sighed.

His hands moved up my back and tangled in my hair, his tongue found mine. His thumb rubbed over the sensitive area behind my ear and I moaned.

He sat up, his arms wrapping around me to steady me before he tugged my shirt over my head, got rid of my bra and put me on the floor where he'd been.

His lips traced along my jawline, down my neck, and across my collarbone. He left slow, sensual kisses over my skin.

Goosebumps covered my body.

I arched into him as he sucked a nipple into his mouth, his tongue swirling over it. Heat pooled between my legs. I grabbed fistfuls of his hair as he moved to the other breast.

He kissed and licked his way down my belly until he reached the waist of my jeans. His eyes flicked up to mine, his fingers getting to work on the button when I nodded.

Laying naked while he took me in, I should have been shy, or even self-conscious after all this time, but I wasn't.

His eyes fell on the small tattoo of Jughead's hat on my hip and he smiled.

"Any more?" he asked.

I shook my head.

He knelt between my legs, his lips finding the small hat, and I shivered.

I'd missed those hands, that mouth…

Mason lay down and hooked my legs over his shoulders, his strong hands taking a hold of my hips. His tongue pushed into me and I groaned.

That tongue.

It had been a while since I'd been with someone and I'd yet to be with anyone who was as attentive as Mason.

He replaced his tongue with his fingers. He curled them, stoking the fire building in me. The pressure was building and my legs started to shake.

"Mason…"

He quickened his strokes, his tongue lapping over my clit. I jerked against him, panting.

"Mace…" I needed him. I wanted him…

He did that thing with his tongue. That slow roll that pushed me over the edge every single time.

My knees clenched around his head, my fingers digging into his hair, as wave after wave of pleasure rolled through me.

Mason kept up his assault until I was a boneless mess on my living room floor. He moved up until his head rested on my breasts.

"Jesus," I mumbled, my arms over my face. That had to be a record for fastest orgasm ever.

I felt him smile, his fingers playing along my ribs.

"Mason."

"Hmmm?"

"Why do you still have pants on?"

He gazed up at me, his hair a mess from my fingers running through it, his lips twitching. "I thought you might need a minute."

His thumb ran over my nipple and it hardened instantly. His eyes darkened at the sight. He stood, stepping out of his jeans and boxers.

He held his hand out and I took it, letting him pull me up.

I took him in. The strong, lean physique, the scars, the tattoos... This wasn't the boy who'd vanished. This was a man who'd gone through hell.

CHAPTER TWELVE
Mason

I stood still as her eyes moved over me, taking in the details. No one saw me like this. I'd learned quickly enough that the scars covering me only brought out the pity, disgust, and fear in people.

I'd almost refused the back rub when Ronnie had offered. I couldn't bear to see any of those feelings from her, but I couldn't hide from her, either. We'd never hid anything from each other until that night.

I stood at ease, my hands clasped behind my back. I closed my eyes, letting her figure out how she felt about what she saw without having to worry about how I'd react.

Her hand on my chest made me jump.

"You're gorgeous," she whispered.

I laughed, surprised, and shook my head. "That's not the usual reaction from people."

Her other hand joined the first and she pressed a kiss over my heart. "That's because they don't see you."

She laced her fingers behind my head and pulled me down to her.

I slowly made my way to the couch, loving the way her hands moved over me.

God, I'd missed her. I'd missed sitting at the library reading books with her. I'd missed laying in the grass and watching the birds eat bread with her. I'd missed spending every day with her, sometimes doing nothing if there was nothing to do. I missed those hands and those lips. I missed those noises she made when I did my best to show her how much I loved her.

I sat and pulled her onto my lap, groaning as I pushed into her. I held her still, rocking my hips until I'd bottomed out.

And I just held her there, lost in her.

"Mace..."

She jerked against me and I started to move, giving her what she wanted. The feel of her gliding over me was intoxicating. I kept her still, thrusting in and out of her. I smiled at the small noises she made every time I bottomed out.

I could feel her tightening around me. Using my thumb, I pushed on her clit, her whimper almost making me come.

I pushed in harder, faster.

Her gasp turned into a ball clenching moan, and I joined her as she clenched around me, her walls spasming with her release.

I stayed buried there, our chests heaving, our breathing hard. I kissed along her neck and smiled at her shiver.

"Let's go to bed," she whispered.

And there was no way I was going to say no to that.

CHAPTER THIRTEEN
Mason

I checked my watch and signaled to move ahead. The tap on my shoulder let me know he was still with me.

In and out. Simple. Fast. Low risk.

I pulled my pack off my back, pulling out everything needed to set the charges. Pup went left. I went right.

Two minutes...

Meeting back in the middle, Pup gave me the thumbs up and I nodded.

Five minutes...

The numbers ticked off in my head.

"Sneak..."

I frowned and looked back. "What are you doing? Let's go!"

He shook his head and disappeared into a hallway to the right.

Three minutes...

I heard a sob and saw Pup carrying a kid. There was no way that kid was more than eight years old. What was a kid...

Pup grunted and the kid screamed as he fell to the ground.

"Contact!" I barely managed to get the warning out before I felt the bullet go through me. "Everyone out!"

Another shot rang out, this time one of ours. My shirt and pants were warm with my blood and I pulled myself up.

"Pup!"

I saw him push himself up, grabbing the kid, motioning for me to go. I turned, getting almost out before realizing something was wrong.

He wasn't behind me. Where the fuck was he?

Bear's eyes met mine before I raced back in.

Pup was down. He wasn't moving. The kid wasn't moving. We had to go!

I stepped towards them and I hit the ground again.

"We gotta go, Sneak!" Bear's voice barely registered.

What were we at? Two minutes? No. One minute? A minute was plenty of time. We could do a lot in a minute... but we didn't have a minute.

Pain. So much pain.

"Mason..."

I groaned, trying to shake the darkness away.

"Mason. Wake up. It's okay."

That wasn't Bear's voice. That wasn't sand and dirt and debris under me...

I let out a long, shaky breath.

I opened my eyes and found myself looking into worried hazel eyes. I sat up, rubbing my hands over my face to rid myself of the last of the nightmare.

Clearing my throat, I shook my head. "Sorry."

Ronnie frowned. "Don't apologize."

"I get nightmares... dreams... they're not good memories."

She lay back down and tugged me down with her.

"They're usually about the day I got my scars... the day Bear lost his voice."

She pressed her lips to my heart.

"I can't tell you where it happened." I took a deep breath.

"Mason..."

"Ronnie... I need to tell you. I want to tell you."

I waited for the objection I hoped wouldn't come. It didn't.

"I was out with my team." I cleared my throat. "Bear, Pointer, Pen, and Pup."

"Pup?"

"Pup was... he was like a dog on a bone... When he got a sniff of something, he didn't let go."

Her hand ran over my chest, giving me strength.

"We... I... it was supposed to be routine. One of the easier missions... an abandoned base..."

Her hand stilled and I blew a breath out.

"Me and Pup... that's what we were good at. In and out. We were quick..."

My voice stuck and I had to clear my throat again.

"I... we were done. The explosives were set, we were leaving..." I shook my head, trying to forget. "The plan was perfect. We had all the intel... the place was fucking empty. I... Pup and I... it was done."

"It's on me." I shook my head. "He caught a bone. He had a feeling and went back...I turned, and he'd found a kid..."

I ran my hands over my face, trying to breathe through the moment.

"I heard the first shot. I saw his face when it hit him. The second shot hit me." I pointed to the scar just off my hip. I heard Bear holler."

Ronnie's hand found mine, her grip tight in mine.

"I couldn't leave him, Ronnie. He was holding that kid... We don't leave family... I lost count. I never lose count."

My voice broke. "I forgot to count..."

I shook my head. "The explosives went off. Pup was right by them. I was a bit farther off. Bear... Bear realized what was happening and was trying to save my ass."

"Pen and Pointer... It wasn't as physical, but still. We all got sent home. We could have fought it, I think, but after Pup..."

I gave her a minute to absorb everything.

I managed a small smile. "Once we all healed up, we decided to set up Pup Security."

"And what does that entail?" she whispered.

"Well, sometimes, a couple of us get stuck babysitting some high-profile rich kid. Not me, obviously, because of the whole hiding from the murdering bastard thing... but a lot of it is setting up security systems, surveillance, and what not. We do some bounty hunting. It was a good way to put our skills to work for us and also set up a legal way to take down the guy who killed my parents."

Her arm wrapped around me and she snuggled in close.

"I'm so glad you're back," she whispered.

I took a deep breath, conflicted. In that moment, I wasn't sure if I should be happy to have her back in my life or terrified that I might lose her too.

CHAPTER FOURTEEN
Ronnie

Mason wrapped his arms around me, but not before I caught a shadow move over his features.

"Talk to me, Mace."

He took a deep breath. "I'm happy. So fucking happy, Ronnie. I can't even come close to describing how happy I am right now, holding you. Since the night I got in my dad's SUV, this has been my end game."

His lips pressed to my forehead.

"But I'm scared," he admitted softly. "I'm scared I got my happy too fast. I'm not done my mission, Ron, and that means he's out there waiting for the moment he can finish what he started ten years ago. It's a game. A really fucked up game, but still a game. It's the longest running game of hide and go seek. The difference between me and him, though, is that I just want him and he's willing to kill everyone I love to get to me."

His arms tightened around me and I tried to calm my heart.

"If anything were to happen to you because of me..."

He swallowed hard. "I'm not going to lie, Ronnie. We're pretty positive he's here because of you. I don't know how he found out about you, but it's not a coincidence he's here. Staying away isn't an option to keep you safe anymore. The best way to do that now is to stay as close as possible."

My heart was about to pound its way out of my chest.

"So, I'm going to take my happy and make sure he doesn't rip it away."

He kissed me softly. "I'm going to win this game, Ronnie. I promise you I will."

He said it with such conviction, my nerves started to settle.

I had to admit, having him back, after the night we'd just had, I'd let the crazy assassin fade away. Maybe it was because, even though Mason had told me the story, it still seemed like an impossible thing. Like Britt had said: it was some crazy movie shit.

I snuggled into his chest, enjoying the warmth.

"I believe you," I whispered. And I did, because if Mason made a promise, he kept it. "What's the plan for today?" I inquired.

"I have to go back to base. A lot of what I do is on computers. I've been scrubbing street cam footage trying to find him."

I frowned. "Is that legal?"

"Do you want me to tell you if it isn't?"

I smiled. "Yes."

"No. It's not legal. Sometimes, if we know who the bad guy is but we don't have proof, I'll work backwards. I hack into their systems and find the proof we need, then we find a way to get to that proof legally. Does that make sense?"

I nodded.

"Bear will come stay with you while I'm gone and Pen is going to come set up a security system for you just to be on the safe side."

I blinked. "Do you really think that's all necessary?"

"I really hope not, but I'd rather be safe than sorry, okay?"

"Okay." I pressed a kiss over his heart. "Do you guys all want to come for lunch? I need to go to the grocery store this morning. I can grab something."

He nodded. "I'm sure the others would be good with it. I'll ask when we get up."

His body rolled over mine engulfing me in a warm cocoon.

Safe. I felt so safe. It seemed impossible that my life might be in danger.

Mason was looking at me, a small smile on his lips.

I cocked my head in question.

"I just... I love you."

My heart kicked. "I love you too."

His lips claimed mine, our tongues finding each other.

I wrapped my legs around his waist, groaning as he pushed into me. He took his time, his strokes slow and deep. I rolled my hips up to meet him every time he filled me.

The pressure was starting to build and I whimpered. Faster. I needed faster.

Mason kept up his assault, refusing to give me what I needed, keeping his thrusts just slow enough to keep me on the edge.

My legs shook with the effort to pull him deeper inside of me.

He pushed off of me, leaving me empty and needy.

"Mace!"

"I wish I could keep you looking like this forever." His fingers pushed into me and I moaned.

He swirled them around until I groaned. "Mason..."

He pulled them out and my core clenched in an effort to keep them there. His hands gripped my hips and rolled me over before pulling them up so that my face was in the comforter.

I groaned as he pushed into me again.

"Jesus, Ronnie. You feel amazing."

Each stroke pressed over that sweet spot inside of me and I pushed back against him.

If I felt amazing, he was perfection.

I was panting, my legs shaking.

Strong hands gripped my thighs, holding me up.

Mason pulled all the way out then slammed back into me.

I shattered.

Pleasure shot through me and I gasped as he kept filling me, over and over until I felt him swell inside me, his thighs tensing against the back of mine.

He gave a few quick jerks before bending over my back, his lips trailing soft kisses along my skin.

When our breathing had gotten back to normal, we headed to the shower.

CHAPTER FIFTEEN
Mason

I sat on the bed and watched as Ronnie pulled her hair up into a clip then put on some clear lip gloss.

Her eyes found mine in the mirror and she smiled.

There was a knock at the door and I left her to finish getting ready while I went to let my team in.

Pointer, Bear, and Pen walked in, the latter carrying a couple of cases that held her security system equipment.

Pointer set down a tray full of coffees. "There's a little cafe on main street. I stopped there yesterday and it is amazing. The owner, Wilma, said that Ronnie always gets a caramel coffee with double cream." He handed said coffee to the love of my life as she appeared beside me.

"Thank you." She took a sip and sighed.

"What's the plan, Sneak?" Pointer handed me a coffee.

"Pen will set up the system here. I'm going to go to base. I have a different program I want to run on the street cam footage."

Every cell in my body was telling me to bring my computers here so I could stay with Ronnie, but I already had programs running and I didn't want to take a chance on missing something if I shut it all down and moved them. What I was going to do was move one of my spares here so I could keep an eye on any alerts if they happened.

"Ronnie needs to go to the store, so you and Bear are with her."

Bear nodded.

Pointer frowned.

"What?"

"Why don't I go with you?"

I shook my head. "I want you both on her."

"Mason, you're his prime target. One of us should be with you."

"No. Logan, I want you both on her."

I saw him think of arguing then change his mind.

"Fine, but fucking be careful," he grumbled.

I nodded.

Ronnie's hand touched my arm and I glanced down at her.

"I'll be fine, Ron. I'm heading to base, I'll be there for maybe two hours and then I'll be back. I'm bringing one of my computers back so I can keep an eye on everything from here."

She relaxed. "Okay."

I kissed her softly. "I won't be long."

She nodded and I gave a wave as I left.

The faster I got the new program running, the sooner I could come back to her. And she'd be fine. The twins would keep her safe.

I made sure to lock the door as I got to base and made my way to my geek lab as Bear liked to call it.

Sitting in my chair, I rolled it over to the computer I used to type in the code I needed. I ran a simulation and frowned. No. That wasn't right.

An hour later, I finally had it doing what I wanted and I sent the command to the other computers.

Now, it was just a waiting game.

I checked to make sure everything I needed was in the case I grabbed that held one of my spares before checking on the active computers one last time.

No alerts overnight. No big break.

I ran my hands over my face.

We were so fucking close.

Where the fuck are you hiding, Bart?

I made him a silent promise. He had one week left to live. He wasn't seeing a pair of cuffs. Coming after Ronnie had been his death sentence.

Taking a deep breath, I headed back to the appartment.

CHAPTER SIXTEEN
Ronnie

Dancing on air. It was a term I'd scoffed at previously, but now, at this moment... I was dancing on air. I smiled as I found a less than ripe tomato in the grocery store.

Mason had gone back to base, and I knew that Pointer was outside waiting for me to come back out. And Bear...

I raised an eyebrow at him as he handed me a riper tomato.

"It will go soft before I use it."

He shrugged.

"Fine. But this one is yours."

He smiled and I tried to look annoyed.

"All right, Teddy Bear. Since you're stuck with me... Do you have a girlfriend? Boyfriend? One of each?"

He grunted and shook his head. He made a running motion with his fingers.

"You're in love with Sneak?

He shook his head violently and pulled out his notepad.

I have to keep him safe.

"So, when do you stop worrying about Mason and start thinking about you?" I handed him a watermelon.

He pointed to me.

I frowned. "Me?"

He nodded. **When you're both safe.**

I let out a long breath. "You know, I'm not some mythical creature who needs rescuing."

He rolled his eyes and pulled a pen and paper out of his back pocket.

Sneak ran into the path of certain death to save one of us...

I frowned, understanding starting to sink in.

"So, you guys are bound to him..."

Bear shrugged.

"He said he ran back for Pup..."

We were all in that building. He ordered us out and ran back in.

I frowned.

He touched his throat. **I was never really big on leaving anyone behind.**

I almost dropped the apple I was holding. "You saved him."

He shrugged. **I was returning the favor.**

"He saved your life before that day?"

He nodded. **A different time, I went down. Shot to the leg. He dragged my ass out of there.**

His phone beeped and he looked at it.

Pen is done at your apartment.

"Jeez. That didn't take her long."

He smiled. **Not the first security system she's put in.**

"And you guys are positive this is all necessary?"

His smile turned to a smirk. He nodded.

"Ok. Well, let's finish up and then we can head back."

I tried to fight off the nerves that were trying to win out. This was crazy. There was no way some hit man was after me. And even if there was, I had four special forces soldiers watching me. Oh, and a new state of the art security system.

I grabbed a few more things and headed to the checkout.

"Hey, Viv."

The cashier looked up as I got to her till.

"Hey, Ronnie."

"How are you doing?"

She smiled. "Good. Thank you so much for Wednesday. I really needed that extra shift."

I reached across the belt and hugged her. "What are friends for? And you know I love Fran. Any time you get stuck, you give me a call."

Just the mention of her daughter's name lit up her face. That little girl right there was Viv's entire world.

I looked back and found Bear taking in the scene.

"Viv, this is Bear. He's a friend."

She blushed and smiled, her freckles jumping off of her pale skin.

He nodded.

"Are you in town long?" she inquired as she busied herself scanning the items.

He shrugged.

She gave him a curious look.

The large man reached for his pen and paper, scribbling something before passing it to her.

She nodded. "Gotcha. I wish I could travel for work." She pursed her lips. "Unfortunately, this bad boy," she motioned to the till, "does not like to go anywhere."

Bear grinned.

Her eyes widened. "Sweet baby Jesus, there's two of you."

Pointer came up behind his brother. "I'm the cute one."

Bear's good humor seemed to vanish and he grunted. I watched, intrigued, as Viv took in one brother, then the other.

My silent friend grabbed a handful of grocery bags.

"Bear."

His dark brown eyes met Viv's light blue ones. She smiled and wrinkled her nose which caused him to chuckle.

She grinned and rolled her eyes. "Brothers."

His lips twitched and he nodded before walking out of the store.

Viv handed me the debit machine. She cocked her head at Pointer.

"Let me guess. Wolf? No. Snake. Buck?"

He laughed. "Pointer."

She grunted. "I thought maybe your parents were really big into hunting or something. Though Pointer does still work for that. You know. Like the pup."

His smile slipped. "No. I don't think either of my parents have ever picked up a gun."

Viv handed me my receipt. "Mom is back from her vacation next week."

"I'll give you a call. You'll need a night out."

She grinned. "Yes, I will."

Pointer grabbed the rest of the groceries and I followed him out to the SUV. I frowned as we got closer.

"Where's Bear?"

Pointer grunted. "Probably went around back to hit something." He shook his head. "I didn't know he was talking to her."

"What was all that about, anyway?"

"It's been that way since we were small. We never understood why, that's just how it is. It was extra bad in highschool. When we were sixteen, there was a girl. She liked both of us; couldn't make up her mind which twin she wanted. I think it was a game to her. I was young and stupid, and I like to win." He glanced at me. "We look the same. I mean, other than the scars we've gotten, we are identical. But temperament wise? Bear has always been quiet. Angry. I've always been easy going, happy. I should have backed down, but I was a kid. Bear's angry side... well, it scared the shit out of her."

He ran a hand through his short black hair. "I took her out on a date and Bear walked into the pizza place we were at. Later, we found out she'd planned it that way. She'd wanted to watch us fight over her. It was my fault. Maybe I wanted her to see him lose it. I don't know. Either way, I didn't hit back. Someone called the cops…"

"So, after all this time…"

He shook his head. "It wasn't just her. And not just girlfriends. Just…" He shrugged. "People. He scares them. Our entire lives… and when he happens to find someone who seems okay with him, they start to pull away when they meet me. It pisses me off when people blow him off. You won't find anyone more loyal than Bear, but most people won't give him a chance. It's even worse now that he lost his voice."

I frowned.

"I love my brother. He's my other half and I'd die for him."

"But…"

"No buts. I just wish more people would give him a chance. Like you."

I smiled. "Your brother is pretty amazing."

There was a grunt behind me and I turned. "Well, what? You are."

I glanced down at his hands, noticing the scrapes, some of which were bleeding.

"Come on. Let's get back so we can clean those up."

I was awarded a smile and nod from the mountain in front of me.

Pointer put the rest of the groceries in the vehicle and we all piled in.

"So, what did you guys decide on for lunch?" Pointer's eyes caught mine in the rearview mirror.

"Burgers, fries, and gravy."

He raised an eyebrow at his twin who shrugged and signed something.

"He says you asked him what he wanted. For the record, if you let him decide what we're going to eat, it will always be burgers, fries with gravy."

"And what do you like to eat?"

"Macaroni salad."

"And?"

He grinned. "That's it."

I laughed. "What about Pen?"

"Fish and chips."

"You guys are going to be easy to keep happy, then."

He shrugged. "If you eat enough survival pack food, you realize those simple comfort foods are heaven."

"Does Mason still love grilled cheese sandwiches?"

Pointer nodded. "With onions and ham."

I smiled, deciding that was going to be our meal next time we were alone.

We pulled up to my apartment. Mason was already opening the door as we reached the top of the stairs.

His grin as his eyes found mine kickstarted a familiar flutter in my chest.

CHAPTER SEVENTEEN
Mason

The grin was instantaneous. There was nothing I could do about it. It had been that way since we were kids. The moment I saw Ronnie, I smiled. She was everything that made me happy. The past ten years without her had been torture, but necessary. I hadn't been sure how I'd expected her to react to me the first time... probably exactly how she had. But this? Now? How she walked straight to me and pressed her lips to mine before going to set the groceries on the counter? That, I could never have dared to dream.

I had been ready to grovel and beg for the next ten years if I'd needed to.

Those hazel eyes met mine and she blushed.

I still planned on groveling. I planned on showing her how much I'd missed her. I planned on spending the rest of my life making sure she knew how much I loved her.

But first... first, I had to make sure she was safe. First, I had to catch the bastard that had somehow found out she meant everything to me.

The only people who knew about my past and my situation were in this room and I trusted them with my life.

I trusted them with Ronnie's life.

The thought that it might be a crooked lawyer or one of the agents responsible for our witness protection had crossed my mind, but none of them had known about Ronnie. The instant my dad had told me what was happening, I'd immediately destroyed anything that might link her to me. Pictures, letters... everything.

When I was done doing that, I'd wrestled my way past my parents and gone to Ronnie's house knowing I was about to hurt the person I loved the most.

It was the one and only time I hadn't smiled at the sight of her. It's hard to smile when your body is trying to collapse under the weight of what you're about to do.

"Earth to Mason."

I looked up from the spot on the floor I'd apparently been staring at and found Ronnie smiling at me.

"Sorry. What was that?"

"You're okay?"

I nodded, smiling to show I wasn't lying. "Yeah. Just having a hard time telling my brain to quit trying to figure out this puzzle for a few hours."

She gave my arm a squeeze. "Come show me how this security system works. Bear already said he was cooking lunch."

I grinned. "Burgers, fries and gravy?"

She laughed. "Yep."

I looked to the kitchen where Bear, Pen and Pointer were laughing at something. "Alright. Let's go."

She led the way to the office and stopped short in the doorway. "That's... That's a lot, Mace."

I looked past her to the four screens now up on the far wall where she'd be able to see them if she was working at her desk. One camera pointed just outside her apartment door, one covered her balcony, one showed her hallway, and the last one encompassed the small entrance on the ground floor with a perfect view of anyone ringing the buzzer to be let in. We were breaking a ridiculous amount of privacy laws setting it up this way, but right now, I didn't care.

Ronnie needed to be safe. The cameras were so small, no one would see them anyway and as soon as I got my hands on the bastard, I'd take them down.

"Okay. So, it's high tech, but user friendly. All the cameras are hooked up to this tablet. You can control if you want to take a picture, you can scroll back if you want to check a certain time. Pen set up the notifications to go to your phone so you can check it when you're out. You can use the pad by the door if you want, or you can use your phone or the tablet to set or disarm the alarm." I walked her through the process then got her to show me to make sure she understood.

Her eyes flicked to me. Shit. I was scaring her.

"Hey. It's going to be okay. I promise. I'm close, Ronnie. I'm so fucking close." Ten years of fear, pain, and sadness hit me and my heart clenched. I was so close. I could feel it. This was where it happened. This was where I finally caught the bastard.

I was just making sure the final showdown didn't happen in Ronnie's living room.

I sat back against her desk and pulled her into a hug, resting my cheek on the top of her head.

Soon. Soon, this would be over and I could just concentrate on Ronnie and what she needed from me to make things better.

CHAPTER EIGHTEEN
Ronnie

The following morning, only Bear arrived while I was getting ready for work.

I raised an eyebrow at him and Mason. "No."

Bear's serious face didn't change. Mason ran a hand through his hair.

"Bear is not coming to school with me." I opened my mouth to say he'd scare the kids, but stopped short, Pointer's story fresh in my mind. I'd meant it more as a reference to his size, but I gave myself shit and reminded myself to do better. "I'll be in a building surrounded by kids and people I trust."

Mason closed his eyes and inhaled deeply. "Ronnie, please. I need to get back to base. I need to tweak the code I put in yesterday. I need to be able to concentrate so I can catch the bastard and I can't do that if I'm worrying about you."

"Why doesn't Bear need to be at base?"

The mountain of a man in question scribbled something on his notepad and handed it to me.

"You leave the geek shit to the geeks?" I burst out laughing.

He shrugged and signed something to Mason.

"He says he'll be bored at base anyway." He shrugged. "He's appointed himself your bodyguard until this is done. If I'm not with you, then he will be."

I grunted. "How the hell am I supposed to explain him?" It wasn't like I could just sneak him in and hope no one noticed. The man was huge. Unless I didn't sneak him in…

"Fine. You can teach my kids sign language. That's why you're there. I asked you to spend the day to show the kids what it's like to have to communicate differently."

Bear's eyes widened and shook his head furiously.

"It's that, or you go hang out with the geeks."

He ground his teeth and nodded.

"Are the geeks that bad?" I laughed.

He shook his head.

"He's nervous around kids. Just hasn't been around a lot of them." Mason gave the big man's arm a slap of encouragement. "You'll do great."

Mason rinsed his coffee cup and set it in the sink. Those amazing green eyes met mine and my heart kicked. His kiss was tender and I sighed.

"Okay. I'll see you later."

He nodded to Bear and left.

"Alright. Give me five minutes and we can…" I glanced at his side. "Do you have your gun on you?"

He nodded.

"You're going to have to take that off. You can't bring it into the school."

He frowned.

"I will let you tag along, but as long as we are in the building, you are not going to have that gun on you. Got it?"

He rolled his eyes, but finally agreed.

I grabbed my things and we headed to work in one of the unmarked Pup Security SUVs. Once we'd gotten in the parking lot, Bear put his gun in the console which he showed me was a tiny gun safe. I saw him check all of the mirrors like he had been doing during the ride here. I scanned the area. With parents dropping off kids, it was hard to see if anyone didn't belong.

Stepping out of the vehicle, I saw Tim stalking towards me. His anger was obvious. I set my jaw.

"You stupid little... You had me arrested! All I wanted to do was go on a date with you!"

"You followed me to a bar after being told very clearly I didn't want to hang out with you. You touched me without asking, and then told me you only wanted to see if I was a good lay. Then you went to grab me again. I didn't get you arrested. You did that all on your own."

His face was an impressive shade of red.

"The officers phoned the next morning and asked if I wanted to press charges. I told them no. Don't make me regret it, Tim, because I can always change my mind."

He opened his mouth and snapped it shut as Bear unfolded himself from the SUV. Without another word, he half walked, half jogged back into the school.

"Think he finally got the hint?"

Bear tilted his head from side to side then shrugged. I agreed. Only time would tell.

I started towards the front doors and turned when I realized he wasn't following. I followed his gaze to the daycare side of the school and smiled.

"Auntie Ronnie!" Fran ripped her hand from Viv's and sprinted towards me in happy four-year-old fashion, every third or fourth step turning into a skip.

Viv ran after her daughter. "Franny, stop! Cars!"

"Fran!" I sprinted towards her as a car left the drop-off line, heading towards the tiny girl who was hidden behind a parked car. Oh god. I wasn't going to reach her. I looked up and saw the same realization cross Viv's face.

A massive shape darted past me and I watched, stunned as Bear reached Fran, his large arms wrapping around her. He turned slightly, tucking her to one side as the driver of the car slammed on the brakes.

Viv screamed as the bumper connected with his other side.

Instead of sprawling with the impact, Bear went with the momentum, rolling, somehow managing to keep Fran tucked against him. He came to a stop on his back after three full rotations, the four-year-old's eyes wide.

Viv knelt beside them, her hands outstretched, but not touching either of them.

Bear sat up with a groan and put a hand on her shoulder. Her eyes darted to his. He put his hand out flat, palm down and lowered it slowly.

Calm. He was telling her to be calm.

A little head of red curls popped out from under the crook of his arm.

"Mama? Are you okay?"

Viv nodded, wiping away tears. "I'm okay, baby. I'm okay. You're okay." Her eyes widened. "Oh, my god. Bear. Are you okay? You just got hit by a car!"

The driver of the car looked from Bear to the dent the large man had left in the bumper.

Bear reached into his pocket and grabbed his notebook, wrote something on it, and handed it to me. I read it and handed it to the driver.

It's a school zone. Slow the fuck down.

"Slow the... Maybe if parents could keep their kids under control! My Gabby would never..."

The man's voice trailed off as Bear stood to his full height.

"I'm late for work."

I snorted as he climbed into his car and drove away. The crowd that had gathered started to disperse as it became obvious no one was seriously injured.

I cocked my head to the side. "You're good? You left a pretty decent dent in that bumper."

He nodded.

"I... I don't know how to say thank you, Bear. Are you sure you're alright?" Viv had Fran on her hip and they were both looking up at him.

He gave her a thumbs up and Fran copied him. He smiled.

"You look like a bear," announced the child.

He nodded.

"You can't talk?"

He shook his head.

"That was fun."

He shook his head again then took her hand and placed it in Viv's, his hands engulfing theirs.

"Hold mama's hand?"

He nodded and she returned the gesture.

"Frannie, you know better than to run away from me. You could have gotten very hurt and so could have Bear. Now, I want you to say sorry."

Tears filled her eyes and her bottom lip trembled. "I'm sorry Bear."

His eyes widened as she held her arms out to him and his gaze flicked to Viv's as she passed her daughter over to him.

I was somewhat shocked to see my very protective friend hand her child over to a complete stranger, though I suppose he had just saved her life.

Bear wrote something on his pad and handed it to Viv.

"Lukas." She smiled. "It's nice to meet you, Lukas."

He grinned and nodded. Taking a moment to maneuver Fran so that she sat on his shoulders, he pointed to the daycare in question.

Viv nodded. "Yeah. I've got to get to work, though I have no idea how I'm going to be able to concentrate after this."

He glanced back and gestured with his head.

Oh. Right. Crazy assassin. I jogged to catch up.

I glanced back at the street and frowned. The silver car that had pulled up not long after we had was still there. I caught movement in the driver's seat. Had the person in that car just taken a picture of us? I opened my mouth to say something to Bear, but the car drove away and I decided it was probably a parent checking their phone after dropping off their kid.

Great. Now I was going to become one of those people who saw THEM watching her all the time.

I took a deep breath. I trusted Mason. If he thought all of this was best, I'd go along with it.

In the meantime, I had a class to teach.

CHAPTER NINETEEN
Mason

I ran my hands over my face and blew a frustrated breath out of my nose.

My phone vibrated.

Rat: **She wants to meet.**

Me: **When?**

Tonight. I think something is wrong.

I frowned. **Why?**

Usually, she flirts a little. She uses a bunch of cute emojis. She only used one happy face. I don't know. Something is off.

You want out?

No. I want to make sure she's okay. I know I don't know all the details about the bastard you're after, but I do know you don't hunt down anyone that saves puppies and gives money to the poor.

What?

You hunt down bad people. And this one? This one is different. This one has a special place on your list. So, no. I don't want out. I want to get him before he gets a chance to do whatever it is he's about to do.

This might have been the most I'd ever gotten out of Rat and I stared at my phone.

Okay. You want back up?

No. Don't want to spook her.

Just, be careful.

Always am.

I turned to Pen and Pointer who were cleaning the weapons. "Rat is meeting the girl tonight. He thinks he might get something concrete out of her. She sounded scared."

Pen frowned. "Does he need backup?"

I shook my head. "We don't want to scare her off."

She scoffed. "She'd never know I was there."

"We can't take the chance she has a tail. Rat can take care of himself. He's a big boy."

Pointer snapped the last piece of the handgun into place. "Have you found anything at all in the cam footage you, um, borrowed?"

I shook my head. I'd hacked into the town's traffic cams when we'd first gotten here and my eyes hurt with the amount of footage I had been going over. I'd tried different face recognition software, different algorithms to try and pinpoint any vehicle that looked like the last one he'd been seen driving... nothing.

I glanced at my watch. 2:45. School was going to let out soon and I couldn't get the sinking feeling in my chest to leave. All I wanted to do was go to the school and see her. I wanted to look into those amazing eyes and make sure she was alright.

My computer beeped and I ran to it.

"Holy shit."

Pen and Pointer joined me.

"When was that?" she inquired.

I tore my gaze away from the silver car I'd been looking for and glanced at the time stamp. "Yesterday at 11:04. That camera is just outside of Harold's Groceries." I frowned.

"That's when Bear and I took Ronnie to grab a few things while Pen was installing the security system."

I took a deep breath, willing myself not to panic.

"Pointer, get to the school. I want two of you on her until she gets home then make sure you stay there. Pen, get the gear ready to go. I'll see if I can't track the fucker until he's stopped somewhere we can use."

The pair nodded and did as they were told.

I sent Bear a text. **Stay in the school until your brother shows up. He'll explain when he gets there.**

The next one was to Ronnie. **Stay with Bear and Pointer. Do what they say. I'll be a few more hours yet. I love you.**

My heart was on its way to beating itself out of my chest. She'd be fine. She wasn't alone. She was with two of the people I trusted the most.

I sat at the desk and checked the map, seeing which cameras were in the area where I'd found the silver car. He was one man against the four of us. We had spent the past five years playing hide and seek. This time, he'd made a mistake. He'd come out of hiding.

My phone vibrated. **I love you, too.**

I stopped the footage a block from the grocery store as he popped back into view. He hadn't followed Ronnie and the twins home. He'd headed in the complete opposite direction.

I repeated the process over and over until he passed the last set of lights heading out of town.

"Fuck!"

Pen glanced up, but didn't say anything.

I checked my watch. Almost five. I'd just lost two hours chasing the wrong lead.

I inhaled deeply and reset the cameras to where I'd originally found him outside the grocery store. Backwards. I was going to have to search backwards.

Pen handed me a water bottle and I took a long swallow before I went back to work.

This time, my phone rang and Pointer's name popped up on the screen. Pen's eyes met mine and my stomach dropped.

Something had happened.

CHAPTER TWENTY
Ronnie

I watched as Bear checked his phone and his eyes flicked over to me. I took a deep breath.

"Alright, class. Why don't we practice this sentence? Bears are big and strong."

Bear grunted but smiled.

I was impressed, both with him and with the kids. He'd spent the whole day helping in my class and we'd taken breaks to learn some signs. The kids were picking it up like pros. And for a guy who'd been so reluctant to be around kids, he'd quickly gotten comfortable.

I smiled as I remembered the looks of absolute awe as Bear had filled the doorway before coming to stand beside me.

My phone vibrated and I checked it as Bear led the kids through the sentence.

Stay with Bear and Pointer. Do what they say. I'll be a few more hours yet. I love you.

My heart hit my rib cage and I glanced at Bear who offered me a soft smile. Okay. It was okay. He wasn't freaking out. We were fine. Everyone was fine.

I love you, too.

I concentrated on my class, deciding that worrying about what might be happening wasn't going to help anything.

"Mister Banks? What's the sign for horse?" inquired Lizzy.

Bear showed them and everyone practiced, giggling when they got it wrong the first few times.

We spent the last part of the class learning any and every word the kids could call out. Within reason.

The bell rang and everyone put their things away.

"What do we say to Mister Banks, class?"

My heart swelled as they all turned and signed 'thank you'.

Bear grinned and signed back 'you're welcome'.

"Alright, guys. I'll see you in the morning."

Bear's phone buzzed and he glanced at it before scribbling on his notepad.

Pointer's outside.

I nodded, suddenly nervous.

His large hand squeezed my shoulder, his dark eyes reassuring. Straightening, he cracked his neck and rolled his shoulders.

"Are you sore? There's no way you're not feeling getting hit by a car this morning. I mean, you're big, but you're not made of metal."

He scoffed and signed.

"I'm fine," I translated out loud to make sure I got it right.

He nodded.

"Okay. But, if you need some ibuprofen, or A535, or an ice pack, you let me know, got it?"

I got a thumbs up.

Outside, Pointer visibly relaxed at the sight of us.

"Did you notice a silver car today?" he asked his brother.

Bear thought back and signed 'maybe'.

"I did. This morning. It was sitting on the street right about the time you got hit by the car."

Pointer raised an eyebrow, but left his questions unasked for the time being.

The twins both turned their attention to our surroundings and I tried to see if I could recognize the car again. Nothing.

"I'm parked beside you. We'll play shell game."

Bear nodded.

I had no idea what shell game was, but I followed the wall of brothers until we reached the SUVs. They opened all four doors between the two vehicles, Bear at the front and Pointer at the back. They let me in the middle.

"Get into mine. Sit in the back." Pointer was watching the parking lot.

I glanced at Bear who nodded. I stayed as low as possible, crawling into the driver's side and into the back where the windows were tinted. I buckled up but stayed hunched over.

All four doors slammed shut.

"I'll take the long way." Pointer got into the driver's seat.

"What's going on?"

He kept his eyes straight ahead. "Mason found him on the traffic cams. Yesterday, when we were in the grocery store? He was there watching."

My heart was about to come out of my chest.

"So, we'll play shell game. If he was watching this morning, he knows what Bear's license plate is. If he's still watching, he's more likely to follow my brother. Bear will get to the apartment and make sure he wasn't followed. If he doesn't see anything, then it means he followed us. We won't go to the apartment until Bear gives the all clear. If he is following us, we'll get you in the building before he can get close."

"How?"

"Well, for one, he'll be trailing in hopes that we won't suspect he's following. That gives us time. And second, I'll park right on the sidewalk with only enough room for you to get out of the SUV and get into the building."

I pulled my key from my purse.

"How often have you guys done this? How are you so calm?"

He shrugged and checked all of his mirrors. "I've lost count. I'll tell you one thing though; you are a treat to work with compared to some of the spoiled rich kids we've had to babysit."

I laughed.

"Also, there's two of us and one of him. I doubt he's stupid enough to try anything."

I tried to let his words make me feel better.

The SUV's Bluetooth beeped and he pushed the listen button.

All clear. There's construction in front of the apartment.

The nerves returned with a vengeance. He hadn't followed Bear. He'd followed us. He was following us.

"Hey, hey! I can see you starting to freak out back there. Deep breaths."

I did as he instructed.

"We don't even know if he was at the school. This might be all for nothing, but better safe than sorry, okay?"

I nodded.

Pointer swore under his breath.

"What is it?"

"The road is blocked off for the construction. That's okay. There's Bear's SUV and there's no silver car in sight."

He pulled in behind it.

"This changes nothing, got it? You'll stay between me and Bear, and we'll just walk to the building. Easy peasy."

"Okay." I made sure I had everything I needed and got my key ready.

Pointer opened my door and I stepped out of the vehicle. I frowned.

"Where's Bear?"

Whatever Pointer had been about to say never made it out of his mouth. His eyes widened, and he fell to the ground with a groan, leaving a much smaller man I didn't recognize in my line of sight.

I had a fraction of a second to register that Pointer had been tased before a rag covered my mouth and my head started to spin.

The ground disappeared from under my feet and I heard a vehicle screaming to a stop beside me. The door slammed shut.

Then everything went black.

CHAPTER TWENTY-ONE
Ronnie

I woke up, tied to a chair, my head pounding. I blinked trying to get my eyes to focus. I was in an unfinished basement. There were boxes and shelves everywhere. The windows had been covered with blankets.

I pulled at the ropes tying me to the chair and pushed at the gag in my mouth with my tongue. Nothing budged.

"Oh, good. You're awake."

My heart jumped in my chest, my scream muffled by the gag.

The man wore a balaclava, his dark blue eyes meeting mine.

"You know, I knew it was going to take a while to get Mason to pay for his sins, but I really didn't think it would take this long."

A second man appeared, this one also dressed in black with his face covered. This one's eyes were hazel.

Two. There were two of them. He hadn't been working alone.

"Let's do this. It's dragged on long enough," mumbled the second one.

I watched as he set up a tripod and placed a camera on the top. The man with the hazel eyes came to stand behind me, his hands on my shoulders.

The one with the blue eyes turned the camera on.

"Hello, Mason. This has been a long time coming. I'd been hoping to simply find you and end you myself, but it turns out you're quite good at what you do. I'm impressed."

His fingers dug into my shoulders and I yelped in pain, tears running down my face.

"I've been told you care about this one. I'll make things simple. You for her. You come as directed, unarmed. I'll let you know where."

His nails broke my skin and I cried out.

"Don't make me hurt her, Mason."

Blue eyes shut off the camera and pushed some buttons on it. "It's good."

"Give it to the girl. Make sure she's not getting cold feet."

"She won't."

The pair left up the basement stairs and the door closed.

Wait. The girl? There were three of them working together? The man with the hazel eyes had to have been the man in charge. He had to be Bart. Why else had he called out Mason like that. That made him the man who had killed Mason's parents. The other man? I had no idea what he looked like, but his voice hadn't sounded familiar either. I'd noticed he had a slight limp as he'd gone back up the stairs. I needed to try and find a way to get out of here. Hazel eyes had told Mason he'd let me go if he came alone, but I had a really bad feeling that this went beyond just what had happened ten years ago and there was no way either of us were going to get out of here alive.

I started to work at the ropes holding my hands together.

CHAPTER TWENTY-TWO
Mason

I grabbed the empty beer bottle off the table and threw it against the wall, not caring when the pieces flew back to hit me. I tried to get my breathing under control.

He had her. The one thing I'd been trying to keep her safe from all these years had happened.

I punched a hole in the wall and wound up to add another one.

"Sneak!"

Pointer's hand grabbed my arm and pinned it behind me. Bear appeared in front of me, his shirt still off, the taser marks on his body angry. Three. It had taken three tasers to get him down. In the back of my mind, I knew once this was over, he'd bug the hell out of his twin for having gone down after just one shot.

"I didn't know, I didn't know..." Rat was standing next to Pen, her gun at his head.

"God damn it!" I screamed.

I swallowed hard.

Bear's hands moved in front of my face. *Focus!*

Focus. Focus. I had to focus. I had to focus because there was no fucking way Ronnie was going to get hurt just because she was unlucky enough to be loved by me.

I would save her and I would kill him, but before he died, he would tell me how the fuck he knew about her.

Taking a few deep breaths, I relaxed in Pointer's grip and he let go.

Pen put her gun away. "Where did you meet her, Rat."

"At the park, where I always do. But it was different this time. She looked different. Upset."

I frowned. "You were positive something was wrong when you text me. So, what do you mean? How was she different?"

"I don't know. She just... Usually she was cocky. Flirty. This time, not so much. She looked like maybe she was crying."

"Was she hurt?"

He shook his head. "She said... she said she didn't know."

"Didn't know what?" barked Pointer.

"I don't know! She sent me a text, said to meet her at the park. She handed me the tape, said she didn't know, that she was sorry, and ran off. She didn't even take her money."

Pen grunted. "What do you know about her? And I mean everything."

"Her name is Teri. She moved here five months ago. She works at the burger joint just out of town and at the elementary school."

"Wait. What?" I was going to throw up. How had I missed that when I'd looked her up.

"She just started there. Barely a month ago. Part time janitor."

Pointer growled. "She's the bastard's rat."

"How? I don't tell her anything! I don't know anything!"

I fought the urge to punch him. "How did you find her?"

"I was having a burger. She mentioned needing more money... I said I was looking for information on a Bart Kline. I was looking to deliver a court order. I'd tracked him here but couldn't seem to find him. The same thing I say every time! She said she'd just started dating a guy and he'd mentioned a friend by that name. And that's when I let you know."

I blew a breath out of my nose. Was she involved? Did she know what the fuck she'd gotten herself into? By her change in demeanor, I didn't think so.

"Fine. Go. Let me know as soon as you hear from her again."

He nodded and ran out the door.

I sat at the computer and rewound the video. Ronnie's tear-filled eyes tore through me. Her cry of pain as he squeezed her shoulder...

I cleared my throat and rewound it again. And again. I scanned every inch of the screen, looking for a clue.

My heart kicked and I leaned forward, zooming in.

"What did you find?" Pen was right behind me.

I just kept zooming, refocusing the frame until it was clear, then repeating the process.

"What the fuck..." Pointer's exclamation was barely a whisper.

In one of the boxes, a picture peeked over the edge, facing the back wall. A picture that reflected in the mirror hanging there. A picture we'd taken on one of our ops.

There was one marked difference between the one I kept in my apartment and the one I was looking at now. In the one at home, I was grinning like an idiot. In this one, my face and body had been scratched completely off.

CHAPTER TWENTY-THREE
Ronnie

I could hear voices on the other side of the door at the top of the stairs.

"I mean it. Stay the fuck out of the basement." That was blue eyes.

A softer voice answered him, but it was too quiet to make out. I heard a door slam.

I rolled my shoulders, trying to keep them from tensing up. The angle I was tied was terribly uncomfortable. I supposed that was the point. I moved my jaw, pushing at the gag with my tongue. I was not going to die down here and Mason was not going to die trying to save me.

The thought made my heart ache and I pushed it away. No one was dying.

The door creaked open and I stopped struggling.

"Ronnie, it's me."

I frowned at the sight of Teri sneaking down the stairs.

"Teri?" Her name was a muffled groan.

"I'm sorry. I'm so sorry, Ronnie. I didn't know." She started at the knot at the back of my head that held the gag in place. "We have to get out of here. They're going to kill you. Even if Mason does show up, they're going to kill both of you."

I spit the gag out and let it fall onto my lap. "Teri, what is going on?" I hissed as she tugged at the knots holding my wrists.

"I don't know who hates him more, Mark or Bart. I mean..."

We both screamed in surprise as the door burst open and two hooded figures rushed down the stairs.

"Jesus, Teri!" Blue eyes grabbed her by the arm and jerked her to another chair. "I told you what would happen."

"You're crazy!" she yelled at him. She cried out in pain as his palm connected with her face.

His hand grabbed her cheeks and turned her eyes to him. "You were such a good girl, Teri. Why would you turn on me? I told you I'd make it worth your while when we were done..."

"You said it was a game!"

He sneered. "Oh, it's a game, alright. One I'm going to win."

Hazel eyes finished tying Teri to her chair and the pair left. I flexed my jaw, glad they hadn't thought to put the gag back in.

Teri shook her head in disbelief. "I met him online. Mark. We hit it off right away. Oh, my god, Ronnie. I'm so sorry. I had no idea." The tears were still running down her face. "He said he'd set up a game... that it was all some game they all played. I thought it was like that movie where they play tag their whole life. What the fuck is wrong with me? How could I actually

think grown ass men played real life spy games."
She shook her head. "This whole time they were
just using me to get to you so they could get
Mason..."

"Teri, you need to start at the beginning."
She took a few calming breaths and nodded. "I
met Mark on that local online site."

I nodded to show I knew which one she meant.

"He said he'd just moved here and didn't know
anyone. We chatted online for a while and then
we met in person. He was charming and funny...
about a month and a half ago, he told me about
this game he played with his college buddies. He
said they were all tech geeks and once a year, this
happened. Whoever's turn it was would drop a
clue into cyberspace and the others had to try
and find them."

I could see her getting angry.

"He said it was his turn. That he'd dropped the
clue. That I might hear people asking about a
Bart Kline and if I did, that I should play rat.
That I could help him win." She shook her head.
"Idiot."

"Teri. You couldn't have known."

"Really? You would have fallen for it?"

My attempt at a shrug failed. "I honestly don't
know."

"Well, he was right. Out of the blue, this guy
shows up at the diner and asks if I know a Bart
Kline. I'm like, well sure, I've heard his name. He
offered me money to get him information. It was

funny at the time. I'd go back to Mark and he'd tell me what to tell the guy."

She shook her head. "Then, a week ago, Bart Kline actually shows up. But he wasn't funny or charming... he was scary..." She swallowed hard. "That's when I started to think something was off. Then your name came up between them when they thought I couldn't hear and I knew something was wrong."

Her voice dropped to a whisper. "I didn't know what to do."

Tear-filled eyes met mine. "I'm so sorry." She cleared her throat. "I... I heard Mark and Bart talking about a night meeting at the cemetery for tomorrow night... I sent Ray a text and made sure to delete it in case they checked my phone. Mason... he knows where we are."

My heart kicked. Mason knew where I was. He would come save me... I swallowed hard. The thought of him hurt or dead because of me...

"Teri. Scoot your chair this way. We need a plan."

CHAPTER TWENTY-FOUR
Mason

"You're sure the first one is Teri?" I strapped on my vest.

Rat nodded. "She always uses emojis. Even when something is wrong, she fucking uses them. That second one, that's not her. That second one is all flirty and zero emojis. When she's flirty, there's like, twenty of the fucking things in there." He frowned. "Man, I hope she's okay."

I put a hand on his shoulder and he jumped. He wasn't a bad guy... well. Alright, fine. He was. All of our rats were. But he'd served his time, pulled himself out of his bad life and had agreed to work as a rat in an attempt to right some wrongs. This was his fifth job with us and he was definitely our favorite rodent.

"We'll get them both out safe," I promised. "You're sure you want to do this?"

He nodded and zipped a jacket over his vest. "I kind of feel responsible for her, boss."

"Alright. Well, don't go doing anything stupid. Stick to the plan. You go knock on the door. Say you're moving from out of town and you were hoping to look at the place. Your earpiece and mike will be in your pocket. Tap it once for one person, two for two, and so on. Then tell them you'll pop in tomorrow and get the hell out of there. Got it?"

He nodded before heading to his car.

The rest of us strapped on the rest of our gear and jumped into the SUVs.

Pen glanced at me from the driver's seat. "That speech you gave Rat... make sure you practice what you preach, Sneak."

I nodded but stayed staring at the road. My heart was pounding and I took a deep breath to calm it. It was a mission. Just a mission. Enter hostile premises, extract hostages...

We'd done some recon on the address Teri had sent Rat. It was an empty acreage for sale with an older model bungalow. A quick hack of the building permits had given us the layout. We'd also found an old cut across road that came out behind the house. It was overgrown and would give us great cover to reach our objective.

We pulled the SUVs over on the back road and piled out. Hurrying through the trees, we made our way to the edge of the woods by the house.

With the information Teri had given Rat, we were ninety-nine percent positive there were only two men involved: Bart and an accomplice. Ronnie was being held in the basement and, hopefully, so was Teri. There was an old access door to the basement. That was our entry point. In and out. I'd go in with Bear. Pen and Pointer would stay on watch. If anyone tried to get away, they had their orders. Drop them, but don't kill them. I wanted to have a word...

"Going in." Rat's voice was muffled.

I heard two acknowledgment knocks from Pen and Pointer who were keeping an eye on him from either side of the house.

All I needed was to hear two muffled knocks from Rat. Two knocks meant the back of the house was clear and Bear and I could go in. I pointed my binoculars at the door. If Teri's intel was right, there was just the one padlock keeping the door locked from the outside.

"Hi! I'm sorry. I know it's late, but I was driving by and saw the for-sale sign. I was hoping to have a quick look around. I'm new here and was thinking an acreage might be just what I'm looking for."

"Now's not a good time."

"Oh, that's too bad. I'm going on a business trip tomorrow and I'd hate to miss out on this place."

"I said now isn't a good time."

"What's going on?"

"Oh! Hi, sir! I was just telling your husband? Boyfriend? Anyhow, I was just saying how I'm new in town but I'm leaving on a business trip and I was hoping to have a look around before I left. I'm interested in buying the acreage."

Our earpieces knocked twice.

Bear and I snuck to the house, Bear ready with the lock cutters. I wrapped a pillowcase around the lock and Bear squeezed, the sound muffled.

Setting the lock down softly, I opened the door.

CHAPTER TWENTY-FIVE
Ronnie

I sat with my head down, completely defeated. Whatever terrible plan we might have come up with was put to a stop the instant Blue Eyes had come down the stairs and realized we hadn't been gagged. He'd quickly remedied their oversight and tightened the ropes on our arms and legs for good measure.

I heard a car pull up and I glanced over at Teri.

Three deep voices were having some sort of exchange, but they were too muffled to make out what everything was about.

Two shots echoed through the house and I screamed into my gag.

No, no, no, no... please don't be Mason. I pleaded to any and every god I could remember hearing about in high school.

Teri's wide eyes looked over my shoulder and bugged out of her head.

A hand touched my shoulder and I screamed again.

"Sshhh. Ronnie. Quiet."

Relief flooded through me as Mason's voice reached my ears.

"I've got you, Ronnie. You're okay."

His knife made quick work of the ropes holding me while Bear took care of Teri's bonds.

"Ronnie, I need you to listen to me very carefully. I know you're tired, I know you're sore, I know you're hungry, but I need you to run, do you understand? I need you to take Teri and run."

I stood and wobbled as blood rushed back into my legs.

"I can't... you can't..." My voice stuck in my throat.

The basement door opened and someone fell down the stairs, landing at the bottom with a groan. Mason and Bear pushed Teri and I behind them, their guns raised and pointed at the top of the stairs.

Mason swore as someone I didn't recognize started to drag himself towards us.

Teri's hands flew to her mouth. "Ray?"

He looked up at the sound of his name. He nodded and relaxed. "You're okay."

Another shot sounded and he jerked. Teri screamed his name.

"Get them out of here, Bear." Mason's voice left no room for discussion. "Ronnie, you follow him and do exactly what he says." He reached back with one hand and squeezed mine, his eyes still on the stairs.

Bear grunted and jerked his head toward the door behind us.

"I..." I cleared my throat. "Please be careful."

He gave one short nod.

I grabbed Teri's hand. "Come on, Teri."

Bear pointed to the woods.

"Straight?"

He nodded.

I glanced back to see Mason one last time before we sprinted into the woods.

CHAPTER TWENTY-SIX
Mason

I took a deep breath and let myself feel relief for a fraction of a second as Bear got the girls out of the basement. Whatever happened now, at least Ronnie was safe.

"They're going out the back!"

Bart's voice from upstairs made my skin crawl.

I heard running over my head, the front door slam open, and a shot rang through the air.

A scoff sounded down the stairway.

"Idiot."

I felt the blood drain from my face and a wave of dizziness hit me. I shook my head to refocus. There was no way...

"I'm going to assume you're still down there, Mason. I'm coming down."

My stomach rolled at the sight of Pup stepping into view, his gun pointed at me.

"Mark?"

He chuckled. "Man, you should see your face right now."

"I..." I started to lower my gun, then stopped. This man had just kidnapped the woman I loved and was working with the bastard that had killed my parents. "We thought you died!"

Pup grunted. "You left me there to die."

I shook my head. "I went back in. I tried to get to you."

Memories from that day slammed into me. His body and the boy's laying in a pool of blood. The pain. The darkness...

"I almost got to you..."

"I saw you run, you lying piece of shit!" He stepped over Rat's body.

"You were right behind me!"

"But I wasn't, was I?"

I shook my head. "I saw you weren't. I went back in. Bear... Bear went back in with me."

"Bullshit!"

"Jesus, Mark! We both got caught in the blast. Bear's throat got crushed. He can't talk anymore. If it wasn't for Pointer pulling me out from under a wall when he did, I'd be dead." I inhaled deeply, calming myself. "There was nothing left of the building. Where you were laying when the blast happened... There was nothing left..."

"I was left!" he yelled. "I was under there! I was under there for two days!"

I shook my head. "They sent a crew back. They said they sent a crew back... They said there was nothing left." I swallowed hard. "How? How did you get out?"

"That kid's family."

"Did he..."

"No." His eyes narrowed. "They dug us up. I spent a year in that fucking hell hole trying to heal. I lost my leg! And the whole fucking time, I thought, they'll come back. They'll come for me. There's no way they'd just leave me here... turns out I was wrong."

"We got sent home. You were dead." I had to clear my throat. "If we'd even thought for a half second you were still alive, we never would have left. You know that. We had a fucking funeral for Christ's sakes!"

He shook his head. "I had a year. A year to figure out what I was going to do when I got back. At first, I was just going to show up and say, surprise! But the longer I stayed there, the more I realized that wouldn't do. A year of pain and nightmares and of being alone... You have no idea the terror I felt..."

A slight movement behind him caught my eye. Rat. Rat was still alive.

Pup shrugged. "So, I made a plan. Find your girlfriend. That was easy enough. You never shut up about her. Get word to Bart... that part was easy. I sent one email with your name on it and he was all over it. And then wait for you to come to me..."

"Why Ronnie? Why involve her?"

"Because I lost everything... and you were going to feel what that felt like before I killed you." He smirked. "Oh well. I suppose this is close enough. You'll just have to die knowing that one by one, they're all going to feel that fear. The fear of being trapped right before I put a bullet in their heads."

I felt the bullet cut through my arm before I heard the blast. The second shot hit my vest. The impact sent me falling, my gun slipping from my grasp. Mark took a few steps towards me, his face red, his eyes wild. In the corner of my eye, I saw Rat reach for the gun he'd put in the waist of his pants under his jacket. He rolled and fired as I pulled my handgun from its holster, firing into Pup's chest.

Mark dropped his gun as bullets hit him from the front and the back. I kicked it away.

Rat stumbled to his feet and ran towards us.

I got up, my gun on Pup.

"This is going to be like old times, Sneak." The words pushed blood past his lips.

Rat slammed into me as Pup dropped the grenade, the blast sending both of us sprawling through the air, pushing us out the door.

CHAPTER TWENTY-SEVEN
Ronnie

I stopped short and turned at the sound of the explosion, my heart in my throat.

Bear grunted and I looked up into his wide eyes. He put a hand up and pointed towards the SUVs we'd just reached.

"I can't just sit here, Lukas! You'll need to help if they're hurt!"

His jaw tightened. He took a fraction of a second before nodding. He grabbed his pad and pen from a pocket on his vest.

You stay behind me and you do not move unless I tell you. Are we clear? He showed both Teri and I the paper.

I nodded. "Promise."

Another gunshot rang through the air and I let a slow shaking breath out of my nose.

Bear put a hand to his ear then clicked once on his radio.

Shot = Bart dead

He motioned for us to follow him. Teri hesitated a fraction of a second before falling into step behind us.

The scene before us as we emerged from the trees was heart wrenching. Most of the house had collapsed. Pointer was doing CPR on Rat. Pen was on her phone, holding pressure on a wound on the side of Mason's head. He wasn't moving.

"Look, you small town idiot. If you ask me one more time what we were doing here, I'm going to reach through the phone and choke the fucking life out of you. Check with your captain. We had his permission. Now get the fucking ambulance here now!" She threw her phone to the ground and straddled Mason to keep him still when he moaned and started to move.

"Ron..." My name was barely a mumble.

I ran to his side, tears streaming down my face. "I'm here, Mace. I'm good. You're good. Just lay still..." I pressed my lips to his forehead and took his hand gently in mine, unsure of where he might be hurt.

Stroking his face, letting him know I was there, I looked up to where Bear and Pointer were still working on Rat. Terri stood out of the way, her hands over her mouth.

Rat gasped and the twins sat up, watching to see if they needed to keep going. Bear checked his pulse and nodded, giving Teri a thumbs up. Pointer turned his attention to stopping the bleeding from the man's right arm while Bear moved to the piece of wood protruding from Rat's leg.

Teri knelt beside him and took his hand.

Mason groaned Rat's name.

"He's alive," I reassured him. "Bear and Pointer are with him."

"Pup…"

Pen took a deep breath and swallowed hard. "Gone for good, this time. I couldn't pull him out. There's not enough left of him to check for a pulse."

She looked at my surprise. "We all heard over the radio."

We all looked up at the lights and sirens coming up the driveway.

She offered me a reassuring smile. "I'll fill you in later."

I nodded and stepped back as the paramedics moved in with stretchers and medical gear.

A police cruiser pulled up, the officer stepping out and walking over.

She frowned at the scene. "I'm going to need your weapons and you'll all need to come down to the station."

Pen scoffed. "Yeah. No. That's not happening. We're going to the hospital to make sure our team makes it out whole."

The woman's eyes met mine and she frowned. "Ronnie?"

I blinked. "Oh! Ginny! I'm sorry. I didn't… With everything…" I waved at the scene around us. "Can you… could you maybe let Lizzy know she'll have a substitute tomorrow? I know she hates surprises…"

She gawked at me. "What are you doing here?"

"I... I was taken hostage. These guys saved me. They're the good guys here."

"Jesus. Okay." She turned to Pen. "Give me the weapons you fired. We'll deal with the rest later."

She handed her the rifle on the ground.

"That's it?" she inquired, looking at the carnage.

"You don't need more than that when you're as good as me, sweetheart. And I had nothing to do with this. I took out the one out front."

Pen handed her Rat's and Mason's guns. "There were shots inside, but I have no idea who shot what. There's a body in the rubble. There should be at least two more guns in there too."

Pointer walked up with Bear as they loaded Rat into the ambulance. "Bastard would have been mine if he'd turned the other way."

Pen grinned. "It was my lucky day."

Ginny grunted.

I swallowed hard as Mason was lifted into the second ambulance.

Bear squeezed my shoulder and motioned to the woods in the direction of the SUVs.

The time between the instant the ambulance doors closed and we made it to the hospital were a blur.

Teri hesitantly made her way over to us in the waiting room.

Shit. Teri. She'd walked away when Rat had been taken and I'd forgotten about her.

"Did you drive yourself?" I asked quietly.

She nodded. "I didn't think you'd want me along…"

I motioned to her to sit down with us. "You didn't know, Teri. And when you did find out what was happening, you did your best to stop it."

Her eyes welled up with tears.

"Why are you here? Are you hurt?"

She shook her head. "No. I just… Why was Ray there? I thought he was just the weird messenger guy."

Pointer laughed. "Weird messenger guy."

Pen nodded. "He was." She frowned, realizing how it sounded. "He is." She shrugged. "Turns out he's got bigger balls than he let on. When he figured out you were in trouble, he insisted on coming along."

Teri ran her hands over her face. "He got shot because of me," she whispered in horror.

Everyone stood as two doctors came into the room.

"I'm Doctor Willis and this is Doctor Gallager. You'll be happy to know that both Mister Trenton and Mister Duncan should be fine. The bullet wounds were mostly superficial. We've cleaned, stitched, and bandaged those. The most trauma came from the grenade blast. We were told mister Duncan suffered a cardiac episode at the scene but was brought back. So far, it looks like his heart is strong. He has some broken ribs, a puncture wound in his leg and a broken arm.

We're monitoring him and will keep you updated. He's resting, but two of you can go in and stay with him."

Pen stood. "Teri."

Her eyes widened. "Yeah?"

She nodded and the pair followed Doctor Willis.

"As for Mister Trenton," continued Doctor Gallager, "he suffered from a concussion and also has some broken ribs. He's also resting."

Constable Ginny Clark appeared and Pointer stood.

"Go. I'll handle this."

Bear and I followed the doctor to Mason's room.

"If you have any questions, don't hesitate to ask." He shut the door as he left.

Bear squeezed my arm and went to sit in the corner.

I swallowed hard, taking the chair beside the bed. My hand found his and I kissed his cheek. I'd just gotten him back and the thought that he might not be alright...

"Please, Mason... I can't lose you again."

His hand covered mine and my tears turned from fear to relief. I turned my head and found those amazing green eyes on me.

"I'm not going anywhere," he whispered hoarsely. "I'm not ever leaving you again. I promised I'd be yours always. That wasn't a lie."

He pulled my head down with his free hand and pressed his lips to my forehead. His eyes closed and I glanced at the monitors. He was sleeping.

Maybe passed out. Either way, the beeps and blips were steady.

"I love you too," I whispered.

I looked up and found Bear watching us. He nodded before heading back out to the waiting area.

CHAPTER TWENTY-EIGHT
Mason

Ronnie was looking at me, a slight frown on her face. "Mace, are you sure?"

The doctor looked at his notes. "Mr Trenton, I really don't recommend you leave just yet."

I raised an eyebrow. "Look, Doc, this isn't the first time I've been blown up. I'm taking up a bed for no reason. We have ibuprofen at home. Just send me home with the antibiotic I need for my IV and I can do it there for however long I need to."

"Mr Trenton, I can't just let you..."

The machine pumping the antibiotics into me beeped to let me know the dose was over. I swung my legs over the edge of the bed, hiding my groan. I quickly turned it off and closed off the port in my hand before unhooking the IV line. Grabbing the tape off the machine, I taped the loose end down to my hand.

"Ronnie, hand me my boots."

Yeah. Not my first IV.

Ronnie shrugged at the doctor and handed me the boots. "I don't think you're going to convince him to stay, Doc."

He sighed. "You'll be home with him?"

She nodded.

"Fine. If he gets any sort of fever or if the pain gets intolerable, I want you to bring him back." He scribbled on his prescription pad. "Here's what you'll need to finish off his antibiotics and a strong muscle relaxant in case the ibuprofen doesn't do the job."

His attention turned back to me. "I want you to make sure to get up and move around, but make sure you keep the sessions short for the next week. No lifting anything."

I nodded, trying to keep any smart ass remark I was about to say to myself.

Pointer walked into the room. "I've got the SUV parked out front."

Ronnie raised any eyebrow at me and I managed a small shrug.

She grabbed her phone and sent off a text. "Viv was going to stop in and say hi, but I just let her know we're heading to the apartment."

I pointed to the wheelchair. I might have forced my exit out of the hospital, but I wasn't a complete idiot. Walking out was going to be hard.

Pointer wheeled it over and I sat in it. Ronnie grabbed my bag.

"I just want to repeat that I don't advise this." The doctor looked at the three of us.

"Noted," I answered.

Pointer pushed me past the nurses station and I gave a wave. "Thank you!"

I got a few waves and more shocked looks from those there.

At the SUV, Pointer opened the back door and I lay across the seat.

"Good god, Mace, do you really think you should be coming home?" Ronnie's worried face came into view as she sat in the passenger's seat up front and glanced back at me.

"Absolutely. Screw them and their visiting hours."

She blinked. "Wait. That's why?"

I grunted. "Try to tell me when I can and can't see you."

She burst out laughing. "Seriously?"

"I'll heal faster at home anyway. It's a proven fact."

She raised an eyebrow at me then looked at Pointer.

He shrugged. "It's true. You don't get woken up every few hours for tests, there's no beeping machines..."

Ronnie shook her head, but smiled.

I grinned.

The grin didn't last. Every small bump and dip in the road sent pain streaking through my body. I clenched my jaw and breathed through it.

Not much farther, Sneak. Not much farther.

I sighed with relief as Pointer pulled to a stop and I could see the apartment building through the window.

Pen was holding the door open and I walked myself through them. I smiled at Viv who was looking at me like I was a crazy person. She might have been right.

I noticed Bear wasn't around and I made a note to ask Pointer how his brother was doing since the quiet twin hadn't been answering my texts. I knew he was taking the news that Pup had been alive and a part of Bart's plan hard. We were probably going to have to buy a couple of new punching bags by the time he was done with them.

Pointer's phone rang. "Ginny. Yeah. I'll come down and clear that up. You're at the station now? Okay. I'm going to stop for a coffee. Do you want anything?" He smiled. "See you in a bit."

He looked at me. "My statement is hard to read. How about I drop those prescriptions off at the pharmacy for you and Ronnie, you can just worry about getting him settled in."

She smiled. "Thank you."

I noticed Pen watching him and the fact that she barely acknowledged his nod goodbye as he left.

Whatever was happening there, I was too fucking exhausted to deal with it.

Up in the apartment, Ronnie hovered around me as I made my way to the bedroom. I let out a sigh as I settled on the bed and she pulled the covers over me.

She disappeared briefly and returned with a glass of water and ibuprofen.

I took them and took her hand as she set the glass on the nightstand.

"Thank you."

"Of course. Are you hungry?"

I shook my head. "Maybe when I wake up."

Her lips pressed against mine and I closed my eyes, listening to her quietly walk away.

"Ronnie?"

"Yeah?"

"I love you."

I heard her come back to the side of the bed. Her kiss was soft and tender, her fingers running through my hair.

"I love you, too," she whispered before leaving me to sleep.

CHAPTER TWENTY-NINE
Ronnie

I leaned against the doorframe to the bedroom and checked on Mason for the thirtieth time in the past five hours. Pointer had come back with the prescriptions and had explained how to inject the antibiotics into Mason's IV line. He'd said not to worry, Mason would go over it again before it was time to administer them.

I took a deep breath.

I'd almost lost him. Again.

Seeing him in my bed, alive...

I swallowed hard.

His eyes fluttered open and met mine.

"Hey, now. What's wrong?"

I blinked, sending fresh tears down my cheeks. I shook my head. "Nothing. I'm just happy."

He smiled and my heart kicked.

"Come lay with me."

"I don't want to hurt you."

He raised an eyebrow. "Where are you planning on sleeping tonight, then?"

I shrugged. "I don't think I am. I'm just going to watch you."

He grinned. "Not even a little bit creepy."

I laughed and went to the other side of the bed, careful not to bounce at all as I got in.

Mason rolled over with a groan so he could look at me. His hand touched my face lightly. "There. That's better."

His thumb ran over my cheek.

"So, I was thinking you should just move in with me," I announced quietly.

He smiled. "Yeah?"

I nodded.

"I like that thought."

I moved a little closer to him so I could kiss him. Pulling away, I kept my forehead against his.

"Do you think the rest of the team is going to be okay with it?"

"With me moving in with you?"

"Just with you moving here, away from home."

He kissed me again. "This is home, now, Ronnie."

I frowned. "What do you mean?"

"I mean, they always knew. They always knew that once I could get you back in my life that wherever you were, that's where I was staying. I didn't care if you refused to see me and I had to grovel for ten years or if you only wanted to be friends... I wasn't lying that first night we talked. I was back, however you wanted me. The fact that you forgave me for leaving and let me back into your life? I wasn't expecting it, Ronnie, but I am so grateful you did."

He smiled. "A few days ago, Pen and Pointed came to the hospital and told me they'd rented that apartment on the main floor here for the three of them for now and extended the lease on the building we use for base."

He tucked some hair behind my ear. "This is home now."

My heart kicked. This was home now. He really was here to stay.

CHAPTER THIRTY
Mason

I checked my watch. 15:00. Another forty-five minutes and she'd be home. I smiled. I swear I was getting as bad as a dog waiting for his owner to get home after leaving.

It had been almost two months since Ronnie had been abducted and I was getting cabin fever while I stayed in her apartment and I healed.

Now that I could move without nearly passing out from the pain in my ribs, I'd go hang out with the team during the day, but I always made sure to be back in Ronnie's apartment before she got home because that smile? The one I got every single time she opened the door and saw me standing there? I lived for that smile.

I rubbed the towel over my head one last time to get the last of the excess water out of my hair and tossed it into the hamper. I pulled on a pair of jeans and a green t-shirt she'd bought me because it reminded her of my eyes.

My heart warmed. God, I loved her.

Going to the kitchen, I pulled out all the ingredients I had bought for banana splits and got to work making them.

The front door opened and she walked in. I grinned. She smiled and my heart kicked.

"Banana splits? What's the occasion?" She stood on her tippy toes and kissed me softly.

"Well, it's Friday, for one. Second, I've had a good pain free week. And finally, and most definitely the most important reason, is that I love you."

Her smile widened. "I like that reason."

I pulled her in for another kiss. "Yeah?"

Her sigh warmed me to my core. "Yeah."

I took her hand and led her to the dining room table and watched as she took a spoonful of ice-cream and chocolate sauce, closing her eyes as she savored the flavor.

I took a few deep breaths and the butterflies in my stomach started bumping into each other. I could do this.

"So, I was wondering something."

She took a spoonful of ice cream from me. "What's that?"

"I was hoping you'd take the ring I gave you off..." Nope. That wasn't how it was supposed to go.

"Why?" She frowned.

I cleared my throat. "No, that's not..."

She was frowning. I was screwing this up.

"Ronnie, I love you. I have always loved you. I have loved you for so long, I don't remember a time in my life when I didn't love you."

I licked my lips nervously. "I want you to take that ring and move it to the other hand. I want that ring to be the ring that shows the world you said yes."

She opened her mouth and snapped it shut.

"Jesus, I am fucking this up royally. I'm asking you to marry me, Ronnie. From the first day I saw you when I was four until the day I die, I am yours always."

She was just staring at me. That wasn't good. Wait. I hadn't really asked her anything, had I? I cleared my throat. "I... Ronnie, will you marry me? Will you be mine always?"

She blinked and then that smile... Oh, thank God, that smile...

Ronnie slipped the ring from her finger and gave it to me.

"So, uh, that's a yes?"

"Of course, that's a yes."

I slipped the ring onto its new home and pulled her onto my lap. I took a moment to brush some stray hairs behind her ears before kissing her, loving the way she pressed herself against me.

I pulled back and gave the end of her nose a peck. "That was the scariest thing I've ever done," I admitted.

She burst out laughing.

I raised an eyebrow at her. "I'm pouring my heart out here and you're laughing at me."

"Mason, you have been hiding from assassins, been to war, shot at... You have been blown up. Twice."

I shrugged. One day, I'd find a way to explain it to her. One day, I'd find the words to let her know exactly how much I loved her.

Her gaze softened. "I love you."

She pulled me down to her, adjusting so that she straddled me.

And while I waited for the words I'd need to tell her how much I loved her, I decided to make it my mission to show her.

CHAPTER THIRTY-ONE
Ronnie

Those light green eyes I loved so much darkened as his arms wrapped around me and held me in place. Mason's lips found mine, his kisses slow and tender.

My heart was still hammering in my chest from what had just happened. It had come out of the blue. I'd had no idea he'd been about to ask me...

After the initial shock, there was really only one answer to give. What could I say? The man was embedded into my soul.

His tongue ran along my jaw until his teeth nipped at my ear.

I could feel him, hard through his jeans. "You're not too sore?" I barely got the words out as his fingers teased the sensitive spot behind my ear.

All I got as an answer was a grunt. I took it to mean 'no'.

His fingers ran up my sides, pulling my shirt over my head before making quick work of my bra. His mouth didn't leave my skin, making its way down to my breast. The kissing, licking, sucking, nipping...

I groaned, my head falling back as he pulled a nipple into his mouth.

Mason stood and I wrapped my legs around his waist, trying to keep as much weight away from his ribs as possible.

In the bedroom, he set me down on my feet before dropping to his knees, stripping me of my pants and underwear.

His lips, teeth and tongue continued their assault on my breasts, heat pooling between my legs. With one arm around my waist, he pushed two fingers into me.

My hands fisted in his hair as he found that magical spot inside of me.

His slow strokes teased and stoked the pressure building up.

I rocked against his hand, needing more.

"Mace, I'm so close."

"I know."

I opened my eyes and found him gazing up at me, a small smile on his lips.

"You get this look..." He pressed his fingers over my gspot a bit harder for two strokes. "That one. You close your eyes, you bite the side of your lip, your cheeks flush... I'd keep that look on your face for hours..."

I whimpered as he quickened his fingers.

"But then, I wouldn't get to see this look..."

The pressure exploded through me, and I groaned as every muscle in my body tightened.

Mason's arm held me upright until I slumped against him, boneless. He stood, carrying me to the bed, and laid me on it, my legs hanging over the edge.

CHAPTER THIRTY-TWO
Mason

I stripped out of my clothes, loving the contented look on her face. She watched me with hooded eyes, a small smile on her lips. I caught her slight frown as I knelt once again.

I got to work, focusing solely on her clit.

She jerked and I loved the gasp that came as I played with the sensitive nub. Her hips were already starting to move. God, I loved how responsive she was.

"I want to feel you," she murmured as her hands tugging at my hair.

Oh, I wanted that too. But first, I did that thing with my tongue.

Her legs clamped shut on my head, her back arching with pleasure.

Not waiting until she was done, I replaced my tongue with my thumb, keeping the pressure on it as I stood and pushed into her.

The feel of her still coming as I pressed into her warmth was heaven.

She moaned my name as I pulled back and sank into her until I was fully sheathed.

Leaning forward, I kissed her tenderly, slowly rocking my hips.

Her hands laced behind my head, holding me there and I was more than happy to oblige. I nipped and kissed, tasting every bit of her mouth.

She wrapped her legs around my waist, and I groaned as she pulled me deeper.

Her movements faltered and I pulled back to catch that amazing look on her face. I thrust in faster, deeper, loving the small moans and gasps it pulled from her.

Her breath hitched and her release set mine off.

I spilled inside of her with a groan and stayed there until our breathing had evened out. Kissing her one last time, I rolled to the side and pulled her to my chest.

"I love you," I whispered.

She smiled at me, already half asleep. "I love you, too."

I fell asleep thinking of more ways I could show her just how much.

CHAPTER THIRTY-THREE
Ronnie

I took a sip of my beer and sighed, shoulder bumping Bear as he came to stand by me. My eyes found Mason, his grey t-shirt soaked in sweat as he pushed a framed wall up with Rat and Pointer.

"Shouldn't you be over there, Teddy Bear?"

He shrugged and nodded to his bottle of water.

"Yeah. Me too," I laughed.

I looked around the acreage that had once been my prison and smiled. The old farmhouse had been demolished, a new basement had been poured, and today, with the help of our friends, we were putting up the start of our new home.

Yeah. We'd bought the acreage.

A car drove up the driveway and Bear's grin widened as Viv stepped out of the driver's side. She opened the back door and let Fran out of her car seat. The four-year old's eyes scanned the space around her. She took a hesitant step towards Pointer then stopped, kept up her search, and waved enthusiastically at Bear before running towards us.

"Lukas!" The girl took a running leap into the big man's arms and wrapped her arms around his neck.

He nodded and settled her on his shoulders.

Viv walked up with a large container filled with watermelon. She looked up at Bear and blushed.

Hi, she signed.

He nodded again and set his water down before signing.

She smiled. "Someone's nap took a little longer than usual, but we finally made it."

I waited until the wall was secure before handing Mason a drink.

"You look happy," he said with a smile.

"That's because I am."

"Did you talk to your mom?"

I nodded. "The plane took off on time. They'll be landing around eight."

He took a sip of his beer and rolled his shoulders.

"Are you okay? Maybe you're doing too much."

"Ronnie, it's been almost three months. I'm fine."

"You got shot and blown up."

He scoffed. "Barely." His smile softened and he jumped down, his lips finding mine.

I sighed.

"I'm fine," he repeated.

"Okay." I leaned into him, my back to his chest and took in our friends surrounding us.

"Burgers are ready!" hollered Pen from bar-b-q.

Nel handed her a plate to put the meat on. Ginny and Britt pulled the salads out of the cooler and set them on the table.

Everyone gathered around.

"I feel like someone should say a toast," announced Nel.

"What should we toast?" inquired Pointer.

"How about friends," suggested Britt.

Bear's hands moved in front of him, and I smiled.

I nodded. "That's perfect." I raised my beer. "To family."

"Family!"

As we sat to enjoy our meal, I marveled at how things had worked out.

Mason's amazing eyes met mine and my heart soared. I couldn't wait to make up for the ten years we'd missed out on and start working on our future together.

Ready for book two? Here's a sneak peek at
Yours Always, Lukas!

Viv

It had been a week since Ronnie had been
kidnapped and Mason was on his way home. I
buzzed the apartment his team had started to
lease and the door unlocked.

Pen met me at the door.

"Hey! They're not back yet. Come on in." She
brushed her now blue hair out of her face.

Her phone went off and she smiled. "Never
mind. Here they are."

I set the rhubarb pies I'd made on the counter
and joined her at the front door in case they
needed help carrying anything in.

Mason was walking slowly, but without help.
Ronnie had a duffle bag over her shoulder.
Pointer was obviously there to make sure his
friend didn't fall over.

I frowned. "Where's Bear?"

Pen shook her head. "My guess, back at base.
He's been staying there."

"Is he okay?" I knew the jist of what had
happened.

"No. But, Bear is Bear and until he gets out of
his head, there's not much any of us can do."

Ronnie stopped as they reached the elevator
that would take them up to her apartment and I
gave her a hug.

"I made rhubarb pie. They're on the counter." I gestured to the main floor apartment.

"You're the best. Thank you."

"I just wanted to drop them off. Let me know if you guys need anything, okay?"

"Absolutely. Thanks again, Viv."

I smiled until I was outside, and then I couldn't keep the frown from taking over. I glanced at the pie on the front seat of my car. I'd been thinking of dropping it off at Mrs. Brown's since I knew she liked them, but...

I took a deep breath.

Pen had said Bear wasn't okay. That he needed to get out of his head...

I wasn't sure what that all entailed, but the thought of him hurting by himself...

I could imagine that storm in his eyes and my chest tightened.

I put the car into drive and started toward the Pup Security base. I noticed the black SUV in the parking spot as I pulled up.

Music blared inside and I knocked as loudly as I could.

Nothing.

I turned the handle and was surprised to find it unlocked. Letting myself in, I glanced around.

The room to my left was filled with computers, guns in locked cases, and gear. I followed the sound of the music past the kitchen to another room.

I stopped short, almost dropping my pie.

This room had mats, weights, and punching bags. On the far end, facing the wall, Lukas pounded away on one of the latter, sweat running down his bare back. He was covered in tattoos, the largest one of a bear that took up most of his back. Thick legs exited the basketball shorts. There were scars, some partially hidden in the tattoos, some fully visible.

I watched as every muscle tightened and bulged as he tried to decimate his target.

Holy shit.

I told myself that staring was rude, that wondering what those bulges would feel like under my hands was wrong, that wanting to bite that spot just below his ear was...

Feeling terrible for watching, but not wanting to interrupt, I decided to wait in the kitchen. Turning, I managed to bump a chair. The sound of it scraping across the floor seemed excruciatingly loud as the music picked that moment to switch songs.

I glanced up in time to see Bear step sideways and turn with impressive speed. My heart jumped into my throat as I found myself looking into the wrong end of a handgun, the man's face a mask of anger and pain.

The mask slipped, pure horror and regret replacing it.

Lukas quickly set the gun down and turned the music off, his hands and fingers moving as he signed and pointed behind me then to the bag.

I tried to slow my breathing, swallowing the lump that was making it hard to draw breath. I cleared my throat.

"Bear..." His name barely made it past my lips. "Bear."

He was still signing, but I had no idea what he was sayin.

"Lukas!"

His eyes snapped to mine. The storm I'd noticed in the grocery store was back, but tenfold. Those deep brown eyes were saucers in his face.

His lips were moving and I watched them.

I frowned. "Small?"

He blinked then licked his lips before giving a nod.

He moved slowly, his eyes never leaving me as he made his way to a pile of clothes along the wall. Bending over, he grabbed his pen and pad.

Are you okay?

I nodded. "Yeah. I am. I'm sorry. I didn't mean to surprise you. I knocked, but I guess you didn't hear me. The door wasn't locked. I would have texted you, but I didn't think to get your number from Pen..."

His eyes flicked to the corner of the room where his cellphone lay shattered.

"I, ah... I guess that wouldn't have helped anyway."

The storm was still brewing.

"Why were you repeating the word small?"

He frowned and looked at the ground between us, shaking his head.

I reached over and put a hand on his arm. "Lukas."

Why are you here?

"I wanted to make sure you were okay. I don't know exactly what happened or what the history of it is, but I could tell by everyone's demeanor that it was pretty terrible. I stopped by the apartment a couple of times, but you were never there. Pen said you were probably here." I motioned to the pie I didn't remember setting on the chair. "I brought you a pie."

Good, god, I sounded like an idiot. Hi. I've met you twice, but I can't stop thinking about you so I brought you a pie and two minutes ago you almost shot me, but instead of running for my life like a sane person, I have somehow managed to step closer to you so I can touch you.

"Why were you repeating the word small?" I prodded.

He hesitated before starting to write. **It's something I tell myself. It helps when people are around.**

"Helps with what?"

If I think small, if I'm small, they aren't as... He took a few seconds to think about the word he wanted. **Intimidated?**

He underlined the word twice and shrugged one of those massive shoulders. He inhaled deeply and his shoulders slumped.

"Lukas."

Those deep brown eyes met mine.

I don't want you to be scared of me.

My heart broke for him as I read the note. "I'm not scared of you."

I should have been. After what I'd gone through with Dylan, I knew what uncontrolled anger turned into. I should have been terrified to be in this man's presence. I was fairly certain that not much would survive if Lukas Banks ever lost control of the fire storm that was burning within him.

He watched me, looking for any sign that I might be lying.

I moved my hand from his arm and pressed it over his heart. "Lukas, you don't have to be small for me."

His breathing stilled and he managed a small nod before taking another breath.

There was no physical difference in him and yet he seemed to grow before my eyes.

He eyed me warily, like he expected me to bolt away.

Instead, I smiled. "There. That's better."

The grin I got in return was magnificent.

My reminder alarm went off and I clicked it off. "I have to go. Agnes is watching Franny and she has a hair appointment in a bit. If... if you get bored and you feel like it, I promised Fran I'd take her to the park before supper."

He blinked, clearly surprised, though I was certain I was more shocked than he was. I'd never invited anyone other than those in my usual circle to come to park time with Franny. I'd never invited a man to do anything with us before.

"I get it, though. It's not exactly exciting or, you know, most people's idea of a good time, I just..."

His hand on my arm stopped me.

Where is the park?

It was my turn to grin as I wrote down my address. "It's just across from our place."

He nodded then handed me another note.

If you think of something you need before I come meet you, just text me.

I frowned at the number before glancing at the smashed phone in the corner.

He shrugged, grabbed the sim card out of it before motioning for me to follow him to the war room, as I'd come to think of it.

He opened a box and pulled out a brand new phone which he stuck the sim card into.

Our line of work can be hard on phones.

I sent him a smiley face. "There. Now you have mine in case something comes up. Oh, you'll need to put that pie in the fridge."

I couldn't stop myself from taking one last look as he leaned against the door frame and watched me get into my car.

Sweet mother of mountains...

What would it be like to climb him?

I turned crimson at the thought and was glad I was already driving away so he couldn't see my face.

Viv

I've spent the past five years of my life with one thing on my mind: Franny. My daughter is my heart and soul. I'd never really had any interest in men since leaving her dad, but that changes the instant I see Lukas walk into my grocery store. The small mountain of a man who doesn't talk has a storm brewing in his eyes, yet I've never felt safer than when I'm with him. But someone out there doesn't want me to be happy and if we can't figure out who it is, I might lose the one thing I love more than anything... my daughter.

Lukas

My entire life, I've been different; I've scared people. Ever since I've lost my voice, it's been even worse. When I walk into a grocery store and the gorgeous redhead at the till talks to me like I'm not a freak, I have to admit, I'm blown away. When she shows up with pie to check on me a week later, I have to tell myself not to be an idiot. Nice girls like her don't fall for monsters like me. Of course, it doesn't take long to fall for her and her daughter. They're amazing.

When someone starts to threaten them, I make Viv a promise. I'll keep them safe. Because the waste of skin trying to ruin her life is wrong: those two little redheads aren't his... they're mine.

About the Author

Ryenne Renner is a French Canadian author who resides in the beautiful province of Saskatchewan. Wife, mother, author, woods' sprite, food lover; she has many hats she loves to fill. A trucker's wife and mom of three, she is grateful to be able to write full time and stay home with her son with cerebral palsy and epilepsy.

When not writing, her days are spent hiking, fishing, camping, reading, and watching movies with her family.

Ryenne is a romance author who is a firm believer that love is love.

Follow her at the following links!
Amazon:
www.amazon.com/author/ryenne.renner
Facebook:
www.facebook.com/groups/ryennesromancelovers/
Twitter: www.twitter.com/ryennerenner
Goodreads: www.goodreads.com/ryennerenner
Website/blog:
https://ryennerenner.blogspot.com/

Books by Ryenne Renner

Contemporary Romance

Yours Always (Mason, Lukas, Logan, Nyssa, Ray)

Books written as Mireille Chester

Adult:

The Chosen One Trilogy (Crossover, Journey, Destiny)

Holidays in Quelondain (Eggnog Kisses, Candy Hearts)

Ghosts (a Quelondain Short)

Angered Seasons

Crimson Moon Hideaway (Winning Paradise, Feathers Afire, Ocean's Blood, Sweet as Huney)

Sageden Pack (Displaced, Shattered, Strayed)

YA :

Tyler's Story

Chael's Luck

Faerie Dreams (books 1-4)